90 DAYS PROBATION

CONNIE G. BARRETT

FORWARD

Prophetically I have been told that my writing will help a lot of people. Time tells all stories.

DEDICATIONS

Foremost, I would like to thank my heavenly Father who continues to bless me in spite of all my shortcomings. I can truly say that it is through no righteousness of my own that I have made it thus far. To all my supporters, much thanks. I really believe that word of mouth has done more in building momentum for me than any marketing tool out there and for this, I am grateful. To my family, I thank God for you all.

ISBN: 0-9740136-2-5
ISBN: 978-0974013626

Cover by Marion Designs

CHAPTER 1

Todd Henry lie dead to the world stretched out on Joy's sofa. His left knee rested comfortably in the pillow backing. His right leg dangled onto the floor. The uniform ticks of the overhead clock had kept watch of yet another unproductive morning turn afternoon as snarly vibrations exited his windpipe. His bladder, full from last night's 40 ounce, served as his only incentive to face the world.

Wearing a faded black T-shirt and flannel pajama bottoms, he heaved his meticulously cut frame into a sitting position and planted his feet squarely on the carpet. He rubbed the back of his thick neck and yawned deeply before making his way to the bathroom just feet from where he slept. Weak suds formed as he waited for the steady but slow stream to finally come to a halt. He shook himself dry then flushed, the thought of washing his hands not once crossing his mind. He then took a brief glance at his reflection, mainly the contour of his deltoids, before heading for the front door, on his way, taking the liberty of resetting the thermostat well below Joy's acceptable threshold.

The afternoon sun blinded him as he parted the mini blind, yet he still managed a glimpse of the moving truck as it rounded the bend. Kiser's, a locally owned company serving the greater metropolitan area, was his only clue to the new occupant's identity. More than likely, another family, he reasoned, seeing that it was bound for a two bedroom section of the complex.

Windy Creek Apartments had begun as an upscale venture but when the economy took a nosedive, the development company scaled back its original plans, building the remainder of the subdivision with affordability in mind. Their decision to leave out an entire row of apartments and install lighted walkways in its stead softened the stark contrast between the units. Joy's one bedroom apartment faced its better half.

Watching the neighbors had already become Todd's favorite pastime during his going on three month's stay at Joy's. He would scour the premises either from where he stood or from the kitchen which offered an unobstructed view of parking. On rare occasions, assuming Joy hadn't padlocked her door, he took up his neighborhood watch from her room.

It was how he had so conveniently joined Warren during his late morning runs and happened upon his guest pass to the gym, an otherwise off limit amnesty which belonged exclusively to those who paid premium rents. Until last week Todd had taken full advantage of his time at the facility. The day Warren opted not to renew his lease was the same day the office deactivated Todd's guest key. His nearest alternative to a free gym now – the bench press in Joy's bedroom.

Linda was coming up the walkway, returning from her daily walk. She lived several doors down. The units staggered in concert with the landscaping, allowing him to see her come and go. Todd moved closer to the window as the wind whipped her sundress past her thighs. She turned away briefly, shielding her eyes and her three-year-old son who was only steps behind from the debris that the wind tossed about. His breathing was still heavy as he imagined what he would do if he ever got his hands on that.

He was not looking for a relationship, especially not with anyone who was just making ends meet. He only wanted to hit it and quit it, even if just once. But Linda wasn't the type. She'd expect more from him. Plus she lived much too close to prevent her from knocking on Joy's door. The wind died down. Todd stared on as Linda took her son by the hand and went inside. Not giving the moving truck another thought, his mind now solely in the gutter, Todd dropped the mini blind and returned to his place on Joy's sofa.

* * *

By the time Carmen had jerked, tugged and inched her mattress past the entrance, the remaining plastic, joined by duct tape, gave way. The queen size memory foam resisted Carmen's efforts, flipped onto the carpet, and threw her off balance. Exhausted, Carmen followed its lead. Catching her breath, she sank into its firmness and dug her cell phone from her denim shorts.

"Mama, I'm here. I would have called earlier, but I wanted to make sure I got everything off the truck."

"It's going on four. Did the movers get there late?"

"I moved everything myself," Carmen answered cautiously.

"All that heavy furniture? Why isn't Vivian helping you?"

"Because Vivian and I haven't spoken since I told her she had to go." Carmen crossed her fingers then crossed her heart. It was a gesture she performed whenever she lied to her mother over the phone, a gesture to God asking him for more time for her to get her act together.

"When was this?" she asked, not sounding overly surprised.

Carmen winced. "I don't know. Like April."

"I hope you know what you're doing."

Carmen twirled her bangs around her index finger, admiring the length as they unwound.

"The economy sucks all over – even here. They offered me full time. That's unheard of these days. And besides, this place is a lot closer to work."

"That's not what I'm talking about."

There was no doubt in Carmen's mind that this woman should have been a lawyer.

"I'll still get my bachelors by the end of next summer. Don't worry," she assured her. Yet it wasn't enough to deter her mother from carrying out her interrogation.

"I know you're a smart girl. That's never been an issue. Stop letting people use you," she said firmly. "You're too nice. So what really happened, Carmen?"

Carmen rolled her eyes to the ceiling, closing them briefly. "Vivian stopped paying her half of the rent. The lease is up next week."

"And she thinks you're renewing it. So how did you manage to move all that stuff without her knowing?"

Carmen gave in and came clean. "I left most of it."

"Carmen!"

"I don't mind starting over! Really! At least I have my mattress," she said as she ran her free hand along the length of it.

"That's the very thing I'm talking about! Stop letting people get over on you, Carmen! You shouldn't be the one having to start over all the time!"

By now her mother had to realize that the only time Carmen heeded her advice was when she actually asked for it.

"Mama, I got to get the truck back before they close. Love you."

Carmen sat upright and crossed her legs, allowing her chin to rest on her knees as she closed her phone. This was her first day in her new place and she wasn't going to allow anyone to put a damper on her mood, not even Mrs. Viola Daniels. What her mother called starting over, she preferred to think of as downsizing – minimizing her furnishings, her routines, her commute to work, and above all else, her friends. It was only yesterday that she had deleted her Facebook account, all 689 friends, with the same no questions asked aggressiveness that her former hairdresser, Evelyn, used when she hacked off her bangs.

Her mother was a Christian in deed as well as in word. She had never been preachy, just downright persistent. But what she failed to realize was one harsh reality – no matter what you pour into your children, they are not you. Carmen hadn't altogether abandoned her mother's teachings. More than anything, she had placed certain ones on hold for her later years, for when she got things out of her system.

Carmen thought back to when she first left home, when she couldn't wait to get out on her own. She spent her first years on campus, completely taken in by college life. A historically black college. Freshman week. The parties. And the guys. Looking back, she summed up her experience as nothing more than a dorm full of drama queens, oversexed, wannabe divas. Young girls trying to live the lifestyle of the rich and famous, but with cash flows that didn't exist. Always managing to buy new clothes when they could hardly afford to wash the clothes on their backs. There was not a giver in her group – all takers – taking her clothes, her sanitary products, her personal effects. She couldn't keep hair products to save her life. Not even her boyfriends were off limits.

By the end of her sophomore year she was determined not to spend another minute in that hell hole. Between what remained of her scholarships, financial aid and money saved from work study, she moved off campus. Money was tight but she attributed her thriftiness to her mother whom she had watched make a dollar out of 59 cents more times than she could count. Her mother was so good at what she did that her father handed over his paychecks to her like banks hand their cash bags over to Brinks.

Yet somehow the friends she tried to disassociate herself from always managed to seek her out, like Nina for one. Nina had befriended her during her bad hair days. Most of Carmen's hair had broken off from not properly maintaining the perm she fought her mother so hard for before leaving home. Nina, the dorm's self-proclaimed kitchen beautician, talked her into getting braids. Carmen had never cared much for them, especially with Nina jerking through her tight curls with that damn rat tail comb. And they were always too tight, so tight that she kept a headache at least two days after the fact. But in the end, they did prove convenient.

Nina was always showing up at her door along with her daughter. In some ways Nina felt Carmen owed her because in the early days she did her hair for next to nothing, looking for Carmen to provide monetary support she wasn't getting elsewhere, specifically from her baby's daddy. But Carmen didn't see it that way as it was her head that suffered through Nina's learning curve. Nina began giving Carmen unscheduled appointments, every four weeks instead of six. She had also upped her prices, took way too long and to top it off, she didn't know when to leave. The little girl would tear up Carmen's apartment while Nina tore up her head.

Around that time, Vivian asked to room with her. A lot of her reason for giving in to Vivian's request was that most of her "friends" couldn't stand Vivian, especially Nina. Back in Vivian and Nina's home town, they had dated the same guy. Vivian dated him first then Nina took him. After he got Nina pregnant, he pulled a disappearing act. To this day, Nina believes the only reason Vivian transferred was to make her life miserable.

Whether it was true or not, Nina was embarrassed by the situation and did her best to stay as far away from Vivian as she could.

Vivian was a different case altogether. Her masters had to be in manipulation because that heifer sure knew how to play the role of the victim. She lied about everything and had a way of flipping the script on Carmen, making Carmen feel as though she was the one being judgmental and unsympathetic to her needs. In her dealings with others, she was usually the source of confusion, yet somehow Carmen's name was the one that seemed to always pop up in spite of the fact that Carmen stayed busy and was barely at home. Besides that, Vivian never cleaned. She took her stuff without permission, messed up her laptop and was the reason their lights got cut off before finals. She had way too many guys over, using her beloved mattress like some cheap motel. But it was nothing that the right mattress topper couldn't fix, Carmen reasoned.

Carmen laid her cheek where her chin had been. Her bangs followed suit. Seeing how her hair moved and the length she had retained cheered her up. Her hair had been through as many emotional roller coasters as she had, and just like her, it too was finally coming into its own, blossoming for the first time since she had left home. Moving Vivian in may not have been the best choice, but it was her choice. Just as the bad choices she made with her hair had eventually led way to the most stellar care her tresses had ever experienced, so too had her bad choices with people given her the tools she needed to move forward. Her mother's archaic ways of thinking, just like her stiff press and curls, had served her well, but today was about movement - body and shine. And as far as Carmen was concerned, today was all that mattered.

CHAPTER 2

The intense jolt of pain in his lower back forced him to his feet. The moment he saw Joy standing in front of him he cocked his fist, but before the situation could get out of hand, Doug stepped between them.

"I wish you would!" Joy shouted as Doug's huge back blocked her from getting any closer. She had come in from work early and saw Todd asleep on *her* couch wrapped in *her* blanket with the audacity to have *her* air cranked up. She dropped her purse, marched over to where he lie and thrust her high heel in his spine.

"What is wrong with you?" Todd screamed out.

"What you do? Sleep all day?" Doug asked in his usual monotone drawl.

"No!"

"Liar!" Joy shouted as she tried to get past Doug, but his size, serving as a bulwark, kept the enemy at bay.

Doug then nudged Todd toward the door. "Come on, man. Help me carry the drinks."

Todd snatched his wallet off the end table and stormed out with Joy still fussing in the background. He was mad as hell, but his whole demeanor changed the moment it dawned on him that he had not washed his face. His image was everything, but he knew not to step back inside. While Doug locked the door, Todd peeped out his surroundings then lingered a few steps behind, allowing Doug to take the lead as they strolled past the mailbox cluster. That way he could at least hide his face if they happened to pass anyone on the way.

They were both 6'3" and into body building, but Doug, nowhere near as passionate about it as Todd. When it came to eating, Doug's lack of discipline masked the fact that he could deadlift over 300 pounds without even breaking a sweat. Of the two, Todd was hands down the eye candy - lean, well-proportioned and cut from his Murder One down to his ankles with only 5% body fat covering his entire frame.

As they approached the end of the walkway before the sidewalk curved to meet the main entrance, Todd disappeared into the landscaping and quickly turned the sprinkler into a makeshift vanity. As Doug waited for him to rejoin him, the city bus came to its designated stop. Off stepped Carmen, her arms full and nothing but legs, balancing brown paper bags in each arm.

Doug cocked his head to the side. "Damn girl! Look at all that ass!"

Carmen was not the least bit impressed.

"You need some help with that?"

Carmen lowered the heavier of her bags to eye level. She gave Doug a once over, rolled her eyes, repositioned her bag and kept going.

"You one of them stuck up bitches! That's alright!" Doug shouted as he grabbed his crotch. "I got something for that!"

Todd cautiously emerged from the shrubbery, having waited until he was pretty sure that Carmen wouldn't look back and see him with Doug. Doug continued his ignorant display until Carmen was out of sight. Todd, upon seeing Carmen for himself, bobbed his head in approval, the whole while taking inventory.

By the time Todd and Doug returned, Joy had already set the table. Doug sat down first and took another swig from his already half empty bottle as Todd warily sat across from him. A few seconds later Joy emerged from the kitchen carrying two plates on which she had carefully arranged steak, rolls, baked potatoes and salad – all carryout. She placed one plate in front of Doug and the other, she kept for herself.

Todd watched as they began eating. "Where's mine?" he asked humbly.

"You already ate, you greedy ass bitch," Joy said as naturally as if she was talking about the weather.

Doug looked at Todd then at Joy. "Baby, can we have just one night where we can just kick back?"

Joy stared at her live-in. "And can I get more than ten dollars every now and then?"

The way Joy looked at him he knew perfectly well that the next time he opened his mouth better be to put food in it. Doug backed down and returned his full attention to the meal at hand. He was replaceable. He knew who buttered his bread. Joy then rolled her eyes to Todd.

"Todd, we cool, but I ain't yo' mama. You fun and all that, but you lazy," she said forcibly.

"I'll get a job tomorrow. For real."

Todd's pride was bruised more than his lower back. The sad thing about it – next to the sink was more than enough food for another plate.

* * *

Harbor's Staffing Agency was his third stop since eight that morning. He had already endured two long lines of applicants, all without work, all up before the crack of dawn.

Three staff at different times appeared from behind the wood door to take the applicants, one at a time, back to their tiny cramped offices. About ten minutes ago was when the stocky schoolmarm took her last prospect with her. The elderly man, probably counting his days to retirement, hadn't resurfaced in a while. He had only taken a total of two people past the attendant on the other side of the Plexiglas since the agency had opened.

Finally, the door next to the service window opened. "Todd Henry?"

A young blonde not fresh out of college waited for him to walk towards her. She smiled a little too hard, shook his hand and introduced herself before closing the door behind them.

His physique alone screamed disciplined and his appearance boasted nothing short of white collar professional. His choice of the powder blue button down shirt was a natural complement to his Versace's gray two piece suit and Gucci black patent loafers.

She was still smiling when she sat at her desk, but as soon as she opened his folder, she looked totally baffled.

"This can't be right. Your highest level of education is . . . a GED?"

In Mafia style, Todd held out both hands.

"And for the last twelve years, you've held a total of three jobs . . . all less than four months . . . all years within each other. And your reasons for the gaps are?"

Because, unlike you, I'm not cut out to be a working stiff. It's way too much free pussy for that.

It's what he really wanted to say but he opted for, "Employers are intimidated by me. What can I say."

From that moment on, he saw nothing but disgust on her face. Instead of telling him about job openings, she gave a spiel on work ethics and how they were putting their reputations on the line, if – and that was a big IF, they could help him at all. Todd stood up before she could finish.

"You have my number if you find something that suits me."

"Uh – "

"I'll show myself out."

Todd's composure remained calm, but his mind was churning a million miles a minute. Time was running out. His cash flow was nearly depleted and he had burned more bridges than he could count. It was only a matter of time before Joy pulled the plug.

His mind turned to Linda as he boarded city bus 523. Until now, he had kept his exploits across town, far from Joy's meddling. If his situation didn't improve real soon, until he could do better, he just might be forced to hook up with her. But Linda had a child and he couldn't stand kids. Besides, all the money was on the other side of the complex.

He next thought about Carmen. He had taken time out for lunch earlier that afternoon. When he turned to leave the condiment stand, she happened to glance his way. He remembered who she was immediately. As their eyes met, Todd tossed his jacket over his right shoulder, winked at her and left. Carmen blushed as she turned back to place her order. It was a stretch, but maybe, just maybe, if he played his cards right, this new girl, whatever her name was, would be the ticket he needed.

* * *

Even during rush hour, the ambience at Sanford's Roadside Grille was inviting. As Carmen went in to pick up her Thursday special, she saw him again. He was seated at a booth behind the plate glass window and he was eating alone. His jacket lay neatly alongside him. He seemed in no hurry to leave. She pretended not to see him when she got in line, but as she waited, she couldn't resist the urge to look over her shoulder. He had been engrossed in paperwork but he instinctively, it seemed, looked up in time to catch her.

Busted, she thought to herself as she averted her eyes and nervously played in her hair. After waiting her turn, she paid for her order and turned to leave. As she passed him, she couldn't help it. She had to steal one last look.

"You're welcome to join me, unless there's somewhere else you need to be," Todd said as he motioned for her to join him.

Carmen was taken back. "I'd hate to interrupt your work."

Todd neatly tapped his papers together and filed them along with his memo pad in his attaché case. He then lifted it from the table and placed it next to him.

Carmen bit at her lip. "Uh, . . . I guess I can sit for a minute," she said as she sat across from him.

Todd extended his hand. "I'm Todd Henry."

"Carmen Daniels," she said, placing her hand in his. His grip was firm and strong and warm.

"Do you come here often?"

"Actually I do," Carmen answered.

"It's funny how two people can patronize the same business, yet never at the same time."

Even before she had taken a seat, Todd was checking her out, his eyes studiously taking in every detail.

"So is this early or late for you?" she asked, nervously. She liked the attention, but at the same time she was uncomfortable with it.

"Actually it's late. This is one of my usual lunch hang outs. I had a long day at the office," he said.

The way he looked at her, she felt like she was on a speed date. He was scrutinizing, deciding, not worth the time, maybe a good fuck, possibly something more.

"What is it that you do?" Carmen finally asked, after he hadn't said anything.

He chuckled. This time he had been caught. "I'm a research lawyer for Gallagher and Rhimes," he said, sounding as if he'd been forced to repeat it a thousand times before.

"A research lawyer?"

"AKA – flunky. I serve as a repository of case studies and precedents for the hotshots. Nothing glamorous, but it does pay the bills."

"Sounds like we have a lot in common."

"Lawyer?" he asked with inquisitive eyes.

"No. But my head is in books all day. I'm a student at the university and I work for the State Department of Education Training and Assessment Division as a curriculum specialist."

"In layman terms."

"It means I've been traveling the information highway for a long time and I won't be getting off any time soon."

Todd smiled. "Then I'm sure you appreciate leaving your work at the office whenever the opportunity presents itself."

"Yes, I do."

Todd leaned back and threw his arm across the back of the booth. "I haven't proposed . . . yet."

CHAPTER 3

Carmen went inside with Todd just steps behind, her brown eyes carefully taking in every detail. Without even seeing the rest of the house, it was apparent that the living room had to be the largest space in this modest one bedroom home. A weight set and equipment took up a good portion of that. The couch set, pleather, although dated, was nicely preserved. The big plasma screen television, electronics, and the professional blender which sat on the counter of the open kitchenette were all that hinted of any modern day conveniences. The bungalow was on the outskirts of town, on the brink of what many still considered the hood.

"I know what you're thinking. 'He makes all this money and this is where he lives?' "

Embarrassed, Carmen stopped looking around and looked at him. "No . . . well, I mean, well, yeah. Not that I'm materialistic, but – ".

"It's perfectly fine," Todd assured her. "Unfortunately, research lawyers are not on the top of the food chain. Then there was a matter of my college loans that I refused to have hanging over my head. I managed to pay them off just last year as opposed to some of my colleagues who are still paying, some after 20 years now."

"Wow."

"Yes, it's commendable if I do say so myself. And I am saving for a house. Maybe not in the Hamptons just yet, but hopefully somewhere I can lay roots."

"Is that why you don't have a car?"

"How did you guess?"

* * *

Carmen walked along gingerly, carefree, the night air gently caressing her skin. Todd followed close behind at her leisure as she held his fingertips in her own. Last night she had been to his place and now he was coming to hers. When she reached the stoop leading to her apartment she faced him. Even in wedges, Todd was several inches taller than she. He made her feel ultra sexy, even a bit giddy as she basked in the charms of her black Adonis.

All her boyfriends from her past had been just that – boys. She had yet to be involved with a real man. Todd, eight years her senior, was established and comfortable in his own skin. He had been the perfect gentleman as he shared with her his dreams, his plans. She was part realist, part hopeless romantic and he was careful to cater to both sides.

He was working hard at winning her over, in fact, he had never worked so hard in his life. Gluing himself to Joy's window, he managed to figure out her schedule. Each weekday morning, dressed in professional attire, wheeling her backpack behind her, she hurried past the walkway in front of Joy's apartment to the main entrance and caught city bus 1214. Some nights she was in by 6:00, others she didn't get home until close to 11:00. And for two Thursdays in a row, she returned home faithfully with dinner, courtesy of Sanford's Roadside Grille.

By the time he had her schedule down pat, Bobbie's Chicken 'N Ribs offered him a job on second shift. He took it, but only to pacify Joy. He had hardly been there two weeks when he forgot to bring back leftovers. Joy put him out that same night.

By some strange luck, he happened to work with an acquaintance from the same gym he once belonged to. He gave Mario a few pointers for increasing muscle mass. Mario, in turn, offered him the pull out sectional in his house until he got on his feet. Todd had even talked Mario into letting him have the place all to himself for his date, telling him that Carmen was an ex who needed convincing to take him back. Mario consented – anything to help the brother move on with his life so he could move on with his.

"You have fun tonight?" Todd asked, unable to take his eyes off Carmen.

Todd had a way of looking through people, as if they were in his way. But once something got his attention, he studied it. He observed it. It became the center of his world. Carmen had obviously gotten next to him because this is how it had been all night.

"I had a great time," she said, hoping for a kiss goodnight, noting that he had lost his spearmint gum somewhere between the bus stop and the sidewalk to her apartment.

She liked the way his Adam's apple moved when he swallowed. How it accentuated his strong jaw line and the small cleft in his chin. How his voice was so deep, it almost had an echo.

Todd smiled. It was not his strong point. It seemed somewhat awkward. Unnatural. Forced. He hardly smiled. But he was smiling for her. She smiled back, her eyes dancing as her bangs fluttered against her smooth complexion.

"I better head back. The last bus for tonight leaves soon," Todd said then moistened his lips.

As if he was reading her mind, he wrapped his arms around Carmen's waist and pulled her close. She put her arms around his neck and closed her eyes and leaned in as her bangle bracelets dropped to her elbows. His goatee glided softly across her chin as their tongues intertwined.

Todd came up for air and was about to leave, but kissed her a second time, this time longer and deeper than before.

"I got to go. I'll call you tomorrow," Todd said, taking a step back. He finally let go of her hand and walked off into the night.

Carmen went inside and watched him from her window until he was out of view. She then leaned against her door with her head held back and her eyes closed, fanning herself.

Hardly a minute had gone by and Todd was back knocking. Carmen quickly opened her door. Todd stared deep into her eyes like some thirsty blood sucker, awaiting an invitation to come in. A case of *I can't help it took over*. Carmen moved to the side and let him in. There would be no more city buses running tonight.

Todd effortlessly lifted Carmen and carried her to her bedroom. Her bed ensemble was selected with a night like this in mind, only she hadn't seen it coming so soon. Extra pillows and shams sat atop her Donna Karan twilight collection of Egyptian cotton that covered her mattress and new mattress pad. Todd lowered her to the floor then untied her halter dress. She let the crinkle print slide to the carpet along with her bangles as Todd took off his T-shirt and kicked off his cargo shorts.

Carmen felt intimated by Todd as she checked him out. He had the body of a stripper. Her breasts were small and except for her butt, she was more skinny than shapely. What did he want with her? She had worn her strapless bra and matching panties just in case, but felt inadequate and didn't want to take them off. Todd then stood in front of her, placed his hand on the side of her neck and passionately kissed her. As he pulled the clip from her side bun, her hair cascaded to her shoulders, reminding her of how they would do it in movies. It made her feel desirable.

Todd then unfastened her bra, lifted her by the small of her back, and laid her on the bed. He smiled again, reassuring her, as he peeled off the last of her garments. She feared he was one of those muscle men who overcompensated for his shortcomings, but when he took off his shorts, she wasn't disappointed. Carmen sank back into her pillows, her legs sliding up and down his thighs, hoping he made it last forever as he thrust his pelvis forward, rocking her body until he rocked her asleep.

* * *

Carmen crawled out of bed slowly, her senses clouded, still in a stupor induced by too much sleep. It was almost noon and even on weekends, she rarely slept past eight. She looked at the spot where Todd had lay, then reached for her robe to cover her nakedness and hide her shame. Although he had dipped out somewhere in the wee hours of the morning, his scent remained. The residue of sex, no longer a pleasant afterthought, was fast becoming rancid like dirty laundry. Her conscious had returned loud like a shrill bell. No longer beaten into submission, it belittled and condemned her for yet another indiscretion.

Was it something she did, maybe something she said that made her unworthy of even as little as a goodbye? From the moment she heard him walk out her front door, she felt a foreboding of heartache and disappointment take over. He had enticed her to believe that she belonged in his world, when, in fact, he had promised her none of it. No note, not even money under her pillow. At least that would have told her how he really felt.

All that week Carmen suppressed the urge to call him. In fact, by Friday, she thought she had gotten over it. But as soon as Saturday rolled back around, she was on the verge of another meltdown. That's when she finally decided to pick up the phone and call Angie. Angie was her best friend and was very mature for her age, always a voice of reason. Although she was several months younger, she was like the older sister Carmen never had.

"You haven't heard from him in a week? You call his job?" Angie asked after the initial shock of Carmen's confession had passed.

"I don't want to get him in any trouble."

"It would be nice if he felt the same about you! Carmen – you know better."

This was exactly why she had waited so long to tell Angie anything. Although she could talk to her about more things than she could ever begin to discuss with her own mother, she still sounded too much like her at times. It was like getting kicked by a mule from both sides.

"Now's not the time for I told you so," Carmen advised as she was well aware of the consequences that came with unprotected sex.

"You're right. Now would be a little too late."

"You know I have never been one to talk about what happens in the bedroom. But you got to believe me when I tell you he took me to a level that Juan, Trey, Darius . . . not even Derrick could touch what he did to me." She could have thrown out several more names, but it definitely wouldn't help her sound any better. "And I can't even begin to tell you about this man's body. Oh, girl. He was there for me, Angie. Not just to get him some, but he understood me. He understood what I needed. I don't know how else to say it, but he really made me feel special."

"And now he's making you feel like shit. Bottom line: you got played. Really, what do you know about this man? Nothing that counts. This is not the movies, Carmen. Real life is not always glamorous. You should know that by now. It doesn't always have a nice neat ending where you get to ride off into the sunset. This is a college town. These men are whores. That's why you have to make good decisions and you have to stick with them."

Carmen was too nice, too trusting which is why Angie always gave it to her straight. She realized the damage was already done, but she was so tired of Carmen allowing people to run her over.

"So what was it he said that made you decide not to use a condom?"

"That's just it. He didn't say anything. It just happened." Carmen didn't know what else she could say to get Angie to understand.

"And he just walks away like nothing happened. You want me to call him?"

"No!"

"Do you plan on keeping it?"

The question hit her like a ton of bricks. From the time she made the decision to become sexually active, Carmen had always practiced safe sex – always, until Todd came along. "I haven't thought that far."

"I can't tell you what to do, but should you decide to keep it, you basically have two choices. Work full time and put your degree on hold or stick it out with part time and get that degree. Just know that school will be so much easier before the baby gets here. I don't mean to sound unsympathetic, but Carmen, nine months will be over before you know it. You don't have time to feel sorry for yourself. So forget about Todd for now *and take care of you!*"

By now, Carmen had enough experience under her belt to not wallow in it. Angie was right. As bad as it hurt, it was time to get it together. She had serious choices to make and she had to make them fast. No one and nothing had interfered with her education and Todd Henry was going to be no different.

"And Carmen, regardless of whether you decide to keep it or not, make sure you get tested."

CHAPTER 4

She had always pictured herself dressed for a night out on the town and her hair blowing in the wind with her makeup and nails flawless when her future husband popped the big question. Instead she wore oversized sweats, was in need of a shower, and her hair was in a loose unkempt bun when Todd surprised her with a proposal. As soon as she opened the door, she told Todd she was pregnant. His response was *Will you marry me?* Carmen threw her arms around him and cried.

There was no engagement party, no celebration, only an at home pregnancy test. Carmen read the instructions one last time. She then looked back at the results. She moved the stick to make sure the light wasn't playing tricks on her eyes.

From the onset, her menstrual cycles had always been regular, every 28 days like clockwork. It was only when she was under a lot of stress that she might be late, but never off by more than a day. She was overdue by more than a week this time. Her body was already feeling different.

A myriad of emotions went through her mind as she checked the results once again, worried more than anything that Todd would think she was only trying to trap him, out for his money. Carmen took a deep breath and went back to her room. Todd was lying across her mattress waiting for her. He sat up when she came in.

"It was a false alarm. I'm not pregnant."

"You know, I was thinking. We could save a lot faster if we moved in together. My lease is up next month. You graduate next year. We can have a nice, big, late summer wedding. Honeymoon. By then, your lease will be up and we'll have enough to move into our new house."

Carmen wasn't entirely sure why she agreed to marry Todd, but she did, reasoning that a trial run made more sense than diving into marriage head first. Besides, fiancé sounded so much better than boyfriend. If things didn't work, she'd explain it in the dear John letter that would be waiting for him when he got home. Every girl dreams of being a Cinderella, maybe this was as close as she would ever come. That same night, she got her period.

* * *

Carmen was about to get up when Todd nudged her.

"Call and tell your boss you're not coming in today."

"Why?"

"Because I asked you."

"Seriously?"

"I am serious," he said as he began to plant kisses along the length of her neck.

"It's Thursday. The weekend's around the corner," she reminded him.

"Do it for me."

"But I have perfect attendance."

"Come on, Carmen. Do it for me. Please," he begged as he rolled his body onto hers.

The way Todd behaved under the covers, it was apparent that he wasn't taking no for an answer. Carmen couldn't say no.

"Give me the phone."

After breakfast, Carmen peeked around the corner at Todd. He was seriously into his PlayStation.

"So what are we doing today?" she asked.

"Just kicking back."

"We take a day off work to do nothing?"

"Stop being so uptight."

Carmen looked at the back of Todd's head. "Uptight?"

"Let me put it like this," he said, never taking his eyes off his game. "Would you rather be spending the day on the job or the day with yo' man?"

"With you, of course."

"Alright then."

Carmen exhaled. Waking up next to her lover was intoxicating. But if this was what playing house with someone was all about, it was going to take some getting used to. Just so the day wouldn't be a total waste, she spent the rest of the morning catching up on housework while Todd played like some ten-year-old who got to stay home due to a snow day. After cleaning, she watched him for as long as she could stand. She then figured she'd give her mother a call.

"You're home early. Everything okay?" her mother asked.

Carmen crossed her heart. "I wasn't feeling the best. I took the day off."

Todd out of the blue lost interest in his game. Carmen had her back to him when he ran both hands under her top and squeezed her breasts.

"How's Alicia doing with her cold?" she asked about her baby sister as she tried to pull away, holding up a finger for Todd to wait.

"Miserable. It's still in her chest."

"That's too bad."

"Yeah, there's nothing like having a summer cold."

Todd, ignoring Carmen's request, pulled her into him by her waist, ran his hand past the elastic of her sweat pants, and stroked her clitoris.

"Stop."

"What?"

"Wait a second, Mama."

Carmen covered the receiver with her hand as she pulled herself away.

"Wait, Todd." Carmen slowly blew out her breath, taking a moment to get herself together. "I'm back. Oh, nothing. Just looking out the window," she said as she walked towards it. For some reason, actually walking towards the window made it sound more believable.

Todd followed. He jerked her sweats to her ankles, and pushed her forward, heisting her right leg.

"Ouch!"

"You okay, baby?"

"Yeah, uhm . . . I think ooooh, my diarrhea is . . . comin' back! I'll talk to you later, Mama! Bye!"

Carmen dropped the phone and leaned into Todd. No sooner than she had, Todd pulled out.

Disappointed, Carmen asked, "And for that you couldn't wait?"

"And you couldn't tell her you took the day off to spend it with your man?"

"Was I supposed to tell her before or while you screwed me over the phone?" she asked as she pulled her sweats back up.

"Why not? You tell her everything else. Everything but about me."

"That's not true."

"She doesn't even know you're seeing me, does she?"

"Yes, she does. She just doesn't know we're living together."

"My name is on the lease now too."

"When I feel the time is right, I'll tell her," Carmen promised.

"What are you? A grown woman or a little girl?"

"What?"

"You heard me."

"I heard you, but I don't get it."

"You're mama already raised you. I'm your man now. Either you run to her every time life doesn't go your way or you can come to me so we can work it out together."

"Now I'm totally confused."

"You're not confused. You just don't want to admit it. You still your mama's little girl. You got to get permission to be a grown ass woman."

"Where is this coming from?"

"I'm your man now. Not some little boy you bring out to play with then send home when you've had enough."

"I know that. And when the time is right, I'll tell her."

"I'd tell my mama about you."

"Like she'd care."

Todd stood over Carmen. "What you trying to say? You talkin' about my mama now?"

"No, but you're the one who said she could care less," she reminded him.

Todd hit the wall behind Carmen's head. It scared her. Todd then grabbed his keys and shoes and headed towards the door.

"Give me a call when you decide to stop playing grown up," he said before slamming the door.

Carmen quickly opened the door and called after him, but he wouldn't look back.

* * *

Carmen had finally fallen into a deep sleep when Todd came in drunk. He partly undressed and crawled into bed with her. Carmen awoke as he snuggled against her. He then lifted her panties and pushed past the elastic.

"Todd, wait."

"For what?"

"My panties are cutting me."

Todd didn't stop, he kept on like she hadn't said anything.

"You can't wait till I take them off?"

"No."

Todd continued having rough sex with her even after she made it perfectly clear that he was the only one who enjoyed it. The next morning after Carmen got ready for work, she crept back into the bedroom and grabbed her purse, careful not to wake him. Even after last night she wouldn't allow it to become more than just a passing notion, that maybe, just maybe, she had moved a little too fast.

CHAPTER 5

At first glance, she thought she was in the wrong apartment even with Todd having his back to her.

"Whoa!" she let out as she dropped her purse on the floor. *This has to be a mistake! This furniture does not belong in my apartment!*

"Impressed, huh?" Todd asked without even turning to see her reaction as he was heavily involved in his Kinect game, another recent purchase as well.

Concerned was more like it. When she left out for work, the only furnishing in her living room besides a small stand for the television was a silk ficus housed in an elegant ceramic vase that she had purchased as a housewarming gift to herself. It was barely visible now as it had been shoved into a corner to make room for some massive oak entertainment center. If he was going for eclectic, he missed it completely. None of the pieces worked together regardless of how they were arranged.

How could a man that dressed as well as he, who invested a small fortune in designer clothes, have a taste in furniture that was so horrendous? There was absolutely no rhyme or reason for it. The bicolored couch set had standard beige microfiber cushions while the rest of the structure was a burgundy reddish leather. Neither shade was anywhere near the family of colors as her plush taupe carpet. She liked the idea of the round dining table, but country classic – come on now.

The asymmetric glass cocktail table was just downright weird and the three head gold arch lamp, there was no way he could be serious. That thing had to be a throwback from the 80's. She then looked to her right. *No he didn't hang that medallion thing on my damn wall! Is this man color blind?*

Her feelings were seriously hurt.

This crap isn't even fit for a man cave. In fact, that old shit from his house would have worked over this mess. And why on earth did he have to run out and buy another TV when his plasma screen worked perfectly fine?

When she had furnished her first apartment, she bought all of her big items from yard sales where she had meticulously picked each piece. Most everyone who came over thought she had spent a fortune and she received tons of compliments for her sense of style. Of the few people who were willing to help her load the moving van, their schedules conflicted and she was forced to leave it behind.

"I thought we decided to wait until we got the house," she finally said.

"I changed our mind," he said as he air boxed his virtual opponent, delivering a series of jabs to her ribs.

"Without consulting me first?" she asked as she glared at the back of his bald head.

He stopped boxing for a brief moment and turned his head slightly in response to her tone, but still not looking at her. "And how was your day? Glad to see you too."

Carmen immediately backed down. "I'm sorry. I just meant that we have a plan."

"Between the two of us, we make enough money not to be sitting on floors."

"Okay, but –"

"But what?"

"We could of done this yesterday. I mean, I would have liked to have gone with you."

"I picked it out last week. They were supposed to have delivered it yesterday. What? You don't like it?"

Hell, no!

"It's not what I would of chosen, but –"

"It was a going out of business sale," Todd said, sounding more than a little perturbed. "I thought I did pretty good considering most of the stuff had been picked over."

Carmen was disappointed to say the least, but she quickly decided it was in her best interest to be the bigger person.

"You know what? You're right. Why don't we pick up a few DVDs, get dinner and we can come back and see how good it feels not to sit on the floor."

Todd finally put his game down and faced Carmen. Sweat dripped from him as he held her. "Wait till you see our new bed."

* * *

Sabrina narrowed her choices down to two, another modern day romance or switch things up a bit and go with the newly released thriller. As she placed the romance back on the shelf, Todd stood on the other side, looking her dead in the face.

"Long time, no see, Sabrina."

Sabrina's eyes bulged. The DVD she held in her hand dropped to the floor. As she tried to leave, Todd blocked her. Sabrina turned abruptly and fled in the opposite direction as Carmen rounded the corner. Sabrina hit her pretty hard.

Carmen looked at Todd. "She could of said excuse me. That hurt."

Todd shook his head as he held up the DVD that Sabrina had left behind.

"I found one. Let's go."

Carmen and Todd were curled up on the sofa when the door bell rang.

"You expecting somebody?" Todd asked.

"No," Carmen replied as she got up to see who was there.

She peered through the peep hole. It was Angie. She immediately opened the door, greeting her with a hug as soon as she stepped inside.

"Girl, I've been trying to call you. Did you get your number changed?" Angie asked.

"I lost my phone. I haven't had time to reprogram everyone's numbers in my new one," Carmen said.

"Well, I remembered your new address, just haven't had a chance to stop by before now."

As she turned, Angie saw Todd. "I hope I'm not interrupting anything," she said.

"We were just watching a movie is all," Carmen said, joining Angie's side. "Angie, this is my fiancé, Todd Henry. And Todd, this is my friend, always had my back, Angie Grayling."

The announcement came as a total surprise. "Fiance?" she gasped.

Angie extended her hand as she walked halfway to meet Todd. He looked at her as she approached him, but made no attempt to budge for his spot on the couch. Angie stopped dead in her tracks.

"Did I catch you at a bad time?" she asked as Todd looked away from her.

"Not at all," Carmen assured her.

Angie still couldn't believe her ears. "So you're engaged? Wow! When did this happen?"

"It just happened," Carmen said, purposely not going into any details.

Angie turned back to Carmen and grabbed her hand. "And your . . . your . . ." She was about to say ring, but it was obvious from her naked hand that Todd hadn't gotten her one. " . . . your . . . wedding is?"

"Not until next summer."

Angie could tell that Carmen was trying her best to say as little as possible, and Carmen knew the only reason Angie was letting her get away with it was because Todd was there.

"I guess congratulations are in order," Angie said, playing it cool. "Congratulations, Todd."

Todd barely nodded, letting her know that her presence was not welcomed.

Angie then decided it was best to state her business and go before Todd made her say something she might regret. But Carmen would definitely be hearing from her sooner than later, that was for sure.

"Listen. After you left your apartment, all I could do was think about how stupid Vivian would look when she found out you were gone. Girl, not only did I let her have it, I had William to record it for me," Angie said as she opened her purse and pulled out a DVD. "I brought you a copy."

"No you didn't!"

Showing way more excitement than she had for her own engagement, Carmen snatched the DVD out of Angie's hand.

"I got to see this!" Carmen said as she raced towards the DVD player.

Todd cleared his throat and Carmen stopped.

"Oh, I'm sorry. I just got a little too excited."

"No. Go ahead. Have your fun," Todd said. But it was far too late. Angie recognized the game he was playing and was going to school Carmen the first chance she got.

Angie seated herself as Carmen switched out DVDs.

"These first few seconds are nothing," Angie explained after Carmen had sat next to her. "Okay, here we go."

The video focused on Vivian as she walked into the apartment, instantly taking note of William recording her.

"What are you doing here? Where's Carmen?" Vivian asked.

"Hopefully a million miles away by now," Angie answered.

"Away from what exactly?"

"As if you didn't already know. Away from you, you conniving, backstabbing, two faced, no rent paying bitch!"

"I'm calling the cops," she threatened.

"Go right ahead. I'm sure they'll want to know why you're on the premises when your name's not on the lease."

Vivian looked around nervously. "Carmen! Carmen! Come out! This isn't funny!"

Vivian ran into Carmen's bedroom. "Her mattress is gone! Did she move on me?" she shouted.

"Give the girl a cookie. She finally got it," William chimed in.

Vivian came back. "Where did she move to?"

"Vivian, come on now," Angie said calmly. "Do you think she really wants you to know? So you can show your freeloading ass up on her doorstep, bringing all your drama with you?"

"Where am I supposed to go?"

"Ask somebody who gives a damn. It serves you right. All Carmen ever was was nice to you and you took advantage of her every chance you got."

"That's not true."

Angie got directly in Vivian's face. "You are such a liar."

"Get out of my face," Vivian warned.

" 'Bout time! Get her, Angie!" William instigated.

"Or what?" Angie asked as she stepped even closer. "You even so much as accidently let your breath brush against me and I'll whoop your ass in every room in this apartment then post it on YouTube."

Vivian, not knowing how to respond, looked at William.

"Stop looking at me!" It was the best she could come up with before running out.

Todd looked on as Angie and Carmen carried on like two school girls at a slumber party, not the least bit amused by their antics. Carmen replayed the video a second time, setting it to slow motion.

"This is my favorite part. In slow motion," Carmen said. "Look at her face when she sees the camera."

Once again, Todd cleared his throat.

"We just got a little carried away is all," Carmen said as she put the video on pause.

Angie sat up straight. "So . . . Todd, I hear you're a lawyer. Which firm do you work for?"

"You probably never heard of it," he said nonchalantly.

"Try me."

"Gallagher."

"Gallagher and Rhimes. Of course I've heard of them. So you must know Eric."

"Doesn't ring a bell."

"Eric Denton. He's only been there since they opened their doors."

"Oh, that Eric. And how do you know Eric?"

"My aunt used to date him. But that was a long time ago."

Todd had nothing else to say. When Angie saw that his smug ass planned to remain antisocial, she knew that it was time to go.

"Well, Carmen. You know me. Always on the run. I promised to do an errand for Mom. Walk me out."

Todd suddenly stood to his feet. "It's late. I'll walk you out."

"I'll be fine."

"No. I insist."

Todd didn't bother putting his shoes on. He walked to the door and held it wide open for Angie, even before she could finish properly saying goodbye. All the way to the car, Todd was silent.

"These are nice apartments," Angie said, attempting one last time to give him an opportunity to redeem himself.

"Yeah," he agreed. "It's especially nice when you can come home, spend a quiet evening, just you and your woman, no interruptions."

Angie faced Todd as she reached her car. "Is that a hint?"

"If you didn't get it, I guess so. Next time call first."

Angie got in her car and watched as he turned his back to her. She then rolled down her window.

"I forgot to get Carmen's new number!" she shouted after him.

Todd never looked back. He threw out his arms in an 'oh well' gesture as he headed back to the apartment.

"Then I guess you'll have to wait until she calls you! You have a good night, Angie!"

That night after they had gone to bed, Carmen was in the mood for a late night romp. As she made advances towards Todd, nibbling at his ear, rubbing her leg across his thigh, Todd turned his back to her then pulled the sheet past his shoulder. Carmen sat up and looked at him.

"Something wrong? I can't even get a kiss?"

"Why don't you ask your good friend, always got your back, Angie, for a kiss."

CHAPTER 6

The next morning, Todd pretended to be asleep while Carmen got ready for work. He normally was up about ten minutes before she left to see her off. She found herself reading the same material over and over, unable to concentrate at school or at work. She worried all day about if he would even be there when she came back. He had not bothered calling her and she was scared to call him.

The way he distanced himself she wondered if it had something to do with his reasons for ducking out on her that morning she had first allowed him to spend the night. After all, he had never given her an explanation for his behavior and she, not wanting to upset the balance they had finally reached, never dared ask. The more time she let pass, the harder she found it to bring it up anyway.

It was no different when it came to him putting down the toilet seat, washing his own dirty clothes – and his hands, and him passing gas on her when she was sleep – now never seemed to be the right time to tell him how much she hated it. Even their nights out on the town had come to a cease and desist without her questioning him. Although she felt she had let too much time go by to start complaining about some things now, there were bigger issues they still hadn't addressed. Like that STD test. She still hadn't taken it. In fact, he promised that they would go together. It was always in the back of her mind and she couldn't understand how something so important as that never seemed to bother him at all. She hated to admit it, but her mother was right. The way you let a man enter the relationship is the way he will always be.

When she came in that night, he was asleep. She tried to wake him, but he turned his back to her just like he had done the night before. Saturday morning when she got up, he wasn't there. In a panic, she jumped out of bed and checked the closet. From what she could surmise, his clothes were all accounted for. She breathed a sigh of relief. She then checked the kitchen and saw where he had made himself a protein shake as he had left all the evidence on the counter.

Comforted in knowing that he had to come back, she made herself breakfast then cleaned the kitchen, taking extra care to sterilize his power blender to his satisfaction. She then curled up on her favorite spot on the love seat and buried her head in her books. With summer classes being condensed to half the time of that of fall and winter courses, she couldn't afford to lag behind in her studies. Just one day of fretting over Todd had already put her behind several chapters.

When lunch time rolled around, Todd still hadn't showed his face. Carmen decided to take a shower, and let the water clear her head. When she came out, Todd was sitting at the end of the bed lurched forward with his face cupped in his hands.

Carmen hesitated. This couldn't be good.

He's leaving me. I can feel it.

But then Todd looked up and smiled. He beckoned her to sit on his lap. She was more than happy to oblige. As she walked towards him, the odor hit her. Todd had been to the gym and smelled like a locker room after a game. Carmen smoothed her bath towel beneath her before she sat on his lap so that her freshly washed skin didn't directly touch his.

"About the other night," Todd started.

"Yes."

"It's just you reminded me of somebody else."

"You're mother?" Carmen asked, hoping they bore no resemblance.

"I was engaged. Her name was Sabrina. We were together three years. I thought she was happy. I thought we had a future," he said, his eyes were glassy like he was in deep reflection. "But my long hours away eventually got to her. That's when she started spending all of her time with old college buddies."

"But Angie – ", Carmen interrupted.

"Let me finish. As I was saying, Sabrina was hardly ever home and when she was, she didn't want me to touch her. I later found out she had somebody else."

By now Carmen's nose was burning. She dabbed at it twice, but really wanted to just cover it.

With his thumb and the knuckle of his index finger, in the same manner a parent would attempt to get a child's attention, Todd directed Carmen's chin so that she faced him.

"The same way you left Vivian, it was the same way Sabrina left me."

Tears welled in Carmen's eyes. "I'd never do that to you," she assured him as she suppressed the urge to cough.

"You sure about that?"

"Yeah, I'm sure."

"Then prove it."

Todd slid Carmen from his knees to the end of the bed, letting her bath towel unravel as he stripped down to his birthday suit. She tried to look turned on, sexy, but the combination of arm pit and distant skunk wouldn't allow it. When Todd climbed on top of her, she could hardly breathe. As bad as Carmen wanted to, she reasoned that now was not the time to ask him to take a shower. After all, this moment was ground breaking, he had opened up to her, shared his heart, and now that he had, no amount of body odor was going to ever come between them.

* * *

That Monday, Todd had carry out in the oven waiting on Carmen when she came in, Thursday's special, just the way she liked it.

"This is nice. How did you manage to pull it together so fast?"

"I got off early. Thought I'd surprise you," he said as he showed her dessert, cheesecake with raspberry topping.

Carmen smiled. "I'll be right back," she said as she headed for the bathroom.

"Take your time."

"And you ran my bath water. How sweet," she said, shutting the door behind her.

Todd waited for Carmen to finish her last bite before taking her plate to the sink. He then came back with dessert.

"Listen, I was thinking. I want you to go on and finish school."

"Fall semester starts in two weeks," she reminded him.

"No, I want you to go on and finish without having to worry about working too. I got us."

"That's a big step. It's only me and another intern in the whole organization," she said, swirling her cheesecake through streaks of raspberry. "They offered full time to me first. If I give it up, Jennifer won't have a problem snatching it from under me."

"Well, what I was trying to do was save you the trouble of having to take spring and summer classes next year. That way you get your degree in May, we get

45

married in June and we'll be in our new house by July. Right when our lease is up."

"Are we setting a date?"

"It's all on you."

Carmen put down her fork and immediately put on kid gloves.

"You know I want to marry you, I really do, but the economy is so bad right now."

"Then we'll live off our love."

"I got friends who graduated last year . . . at the top of their class and they had to move back home with their parents taking jobs at drive thrus."

"If all else fails, you'll still have me."

"I know, but – "

Carmen knew it was coming . . . any second. Wait for it.

"You sisters! You want brothers to be all romantic, to sweep you off your feet on some white horse and shit and when we do, you take our horse and run us down! And you wonder why you can't keep a man!"

"Baby, don't get mad, please."

"Don't nobody know the future! You can plan all you want, it don't mean nothing!"

"Can I at least think about it?"

"What is there to think about? I'm offering you an opportunity to go on and get through. How many men you know that'll do that for their women? Now, if I was one of them no good brothers, letting you do it for me, you'd be all over my dick. But when a brother decides to make some sacrifices . . ."

For the rest of the night, Todd wouldn't let up. He followed Carmen in every room of their apartment, badgering and belittling her for not trusting him. By the time they went to bed, he was still at it. When Carmen turned her back to him, he kept pushing her and it was making her mad. Everything in her told her to hold her

46

ground, but when he compared her to Sabrina, Carmen
caved in.

CHAPTER 7

Today was one of those rare occasions when Carmen's hair cooperated. Her past shoulder length tresses were at midpoint, between relaxers, where the volume made it look and feel so much fuller. The large barrel iron had given her just the right amount of bounce. With her hair on point, today called for a few special touches: a little peach flavored lip gloss and her gold speckled eye shadow to go with the gold threads in her ruffled print blouse. Her large gold hoop earrings, 18 karats, which she normally wore for special occasions, completed the look. She fluffed her curls with her fingers, turning left, then right. As she gave herself another once over, Todd came in the bathroom and stood behind her.

"Who you trying to impress?" Todd asked, his voice groggy.

"I thought it was you," she said smoothing her gloss between her lips.

"You sure about that?"

"What are you suggesting?"

" 'What are you suggesting?' Always trying to throw them big words around."

"What are you suggesting?" Carmen asked again with a bit more emphasis.

"You never do this for me."

"I've dressed since I've known you. It's just different attire for the office."

"Whatever the man say."

It was too early in the morning for this.

"That's how I get my paycheck . . . and so do you," Carmen said firmly.

She checked her eyes again. There was a tiny smear of too much shadow on her right lid. She took the cleaner side of her applicator and worked on getting it to match her left.

"What's wrong with wearing your hair in a ponytail? Like you do when you with me."

"Right now I'm not in the mood for a ponytail."

"So what you really saying is this ain't about the job."

Carmen looked up from the task at hand at Todd's reflection. "Huh?"

"Do me a favor. Pull it back."

Todd began pulling Carmen's hair towards the back of her head.

"Stop playing, Todd. I don't want to be late."

When Todd didn't stop, Carmen knocked his hand away. "What has gotten into you?"

"Do me a favor. Pull it back," he insisted.

Carmen moved her head away from him as he reached for her again. "I said, no."

Carmen watched Todd through the mirror. Each time he attempted to grab her hair, she moved the other way. Todd then grabbed Carmen's hair and jumbled it all over the place. Carmen pushed him away. As she turned, Todd drew his hand back and slapped her. She stumbled in the direction his hand forced her. The whole side of her face stung. As she reached for her cheek, she gave him the evil eye. Todd stared back, his face daring her to make the next move. Stunned, Carmen grabbed her things and ran out.

* * *

49

The flowers had been sitting on her desk for hours before Carmen finally decided to read the card. *Sorry. You know I love you more than life itself. – Todd*

Carmen tossed the note aside then got up to check her face for the umpteenth time, convinced he had left a mark or that it had swollen by now. She turned to the side, then this way and that as she made another careful inspection. Her reflection bore little resemblance to the happy go lucky young woman who looked back at her this morning. She had thrown her hair in a ponytail on the way there after the wind destroyed what Todd hadn't. Her special occasion hoops, it would a while before they saw the light of day again. All that remained of her confident look was gold dust just beneath her brows. All that remained of her confidence – she'd find out when she got home.

She wanted to tell him to get out and take that ugly ass furniture with him, but each time he called, she lost her nerve and wouldn't pick up. Before today she would never own up to it, but Todd had control issues. Whether this was what drove Sabrina away or whether his behavior was the result of Sabrina leaving, she couldn't be certain. Not even her own mother checked on her as often as Todd. Carmen was always reporting in, telling him how long it would take her to get home, then breaking her neck to call if she was running late. He would even question her about the voices around her, wanting to know who the people were, and if they happened to be talking to her, he always wanted to know what they said. She was always explaining herself. It was never the other way around. It was because their relationship was simple. Todd was the leader, she was his follower.

Carmen touched her cheek again. In the 22 years she had been on this earth, no man, not even her own father, had ever laid a hand on her. If she let Todd get away with it, it would only be two things left on her list that she hadn't checked off.

1. No sex until married.
2. Wait three months before giving it up.
3. Wait at least three months in between relationships before even considering dating again.
4. No unprotected sex unless he's your husband.
5. Never let a man hit you.
6. No married men.
7. Never go down on a man.

To date she hadn't dated a married man nor had she let a man convince her to give him head. For her, oral sex was a no-no. It was just nasty. In fact, her refusal to do it had been the reason her relationship with Trey had ended.

But the more she thought about it, some things shouldn't require a list to begin with. They should be automatic. Allowing a man to hit her and get away with it should have definitely been one of them.

* * *

Todd came around the corner and leaned against the wall, watching Carmen as she cleared the dining room table. He barely said two words to her when he came in. He had gone to the bedroom just long enough to remove his tie and put away his attaché case.

You haven't told your mother about us, have you?"

What is this? Round nine now, Carmen thought to herself.

"I was waiting on my ring," Carmen said, using this as the perfect opportunity to find out why he hadn't gotten her one by now.

"So it's like that."

Carmen held her ground. "The ring makes it official."

"Me asking you should be all the official you need."

Carmen kept her eyes on her work. She hadn't been home long herself. "I go around telling people I'm engaged and the next question is 'Where's your ring?' "

Her only reason for telling Angie was because he was in the room when she came over. If she had introduced him as anything besides fiancé, she would have never heard the end of it.

"See, there it is again. Always got to be about the people. Fuck the people. It's supposed to be about us."

Carmen slammed her towel on the table. "And a ring would let the whole fucking world know that it's just me and you! No fucking body else!"

Carmen's eyes grew wide. She was just as shocked as Todd. Todd then approached her slowly and stood in front of her for the longest time, staring her down. He suddenly grabbed her by her arm.

"What? I'm not good enough for you now?"

"I didn't say that."

"You want some other nigga?"

"Stop putting words in my mouth."

"What you trying to say, Carmen? That my word ain't good enough for you? That we supposed to be like everybody else? Do things to impress these fools who ain't got nothing better to worry about than why you ain't got no ring?"

"Let me go," she demanded.

"I thought we supposed to be deeper than that."

"You're hurting me. Let go."

Todd's grip got even tighter. "So you want to leave now?"

"I never said that."

"Then tell me you love me."

"I love you."

Todd carried Carmen to the couch and threw her on it. The way he whipped his belt from the loops and quickly unzipped his pants, Carmen knew he was really going to put it on her. This man is just passionate she told herself as he began ripping her skirt and panties forcibly from her. He then snatched off her remaining sandal and tossed it behind him as he climbed on top of her.

"Say it like you mean it!" he shouted as he lifted her legs onto his shoulders.

At that moment it meant nothing that her hair was pinned beneath her, her unprotected strands snapping off like twigs.

"I love you!" It was the first time she said it and meant it, with him pulling at her thighs. The harder he pushed, the more determined she was to stick by him. It was times like this that made up for how he talked to her, how he treated her, for when he slapped her.

CHAPTER 8

"**Girl, I love** your hair," Carmen said as Angie joined her for lunch on the patio at Sanford's Roadside Grille.

Angie had her hair in twist outs. All natural. And she was rocking it. Her decision to go natural three years ago had really paid off. She said her hair was stronger than she ever remembered it to be. It was healthy, full, shiny. Carmen was tempted to follow suit, but she didn't have the patience to learn about it or care for it, especially with school and all.

Carmen had already placed their orders since she knew Angie would be running a few minutes late.

"Thank you. And speaking of hair, guess who asked about you the other day?"

"Who?"

"Evelyn. I went in for a wash and a trim. She had the nerve to ask me if you planned on coming back. I told her to expect you on the tenth of never."

Carmen smiled. "What did she say then?"

"She knew not to even go there with me. Her clientele has been suffering so now she's trying to reach out."

"Well, I did rock my hair when it was short."

"But short should have been your choice, not hers. As long as it takes some of us to get length and she decides to chop yours just because. You a good one. Girl, don't even get me started. So how's Mom?" Angie asked switching subjects.

With both their hectic schedules being what they were, they had to move right along, one topic to the next, no time to waste.

"She's hanging in there, trying to keep up with Diane and Alicia. They're talking back surgery for Daddy. He doesn't want it, but he can't keep taking pain medication the way he does. Either he's hurting or he's sleeping. If he doesn't take the surgery, he'll be forced to take early retirement."

"I wish him the best. For all his years working in that factory, he deserves so much better."

"I'll let him know you said that." It was Carmen's turn to switch subjects. "I can't believe it. You are really moving."

"I'll be barely an hour away. My apartment will be ready next week. Can you believe it, two job offers."

Angie was one of the few people in Carmen's circle who was more focused than she. She had taken college courses at her community college while attending high school. She had pushed herself and scheduled her classes so strategically that she only had two courses to take this fall to complete her requirements for her Bachelors in Marketing.

"Have you decided yet?"

"I still need to find out a little bit more about Shoreline. I know what they said about their benefit package, but I'd like to hear it from somebody who works there."

"You know, I believe my coworker's husband works there. I'll ask for you."

"Thanks, I'd appreciate it."

"Are you happy?" Angie asked, wasting no time.

"Uhm. Of course I am."

"So deep down, in your heart of hearts, he's the one?"

Carmen hesitated. "I hope so," she finally said.

"But do you know, Carmen?"

Carmen, already knowing that this talk was coming, had decided beforehand to put it all out on the table, especially since Angie was good at reading through all the fluff anyway.

"I mean, really. When it comes down to it, how well do you know anybody?" Carmen asked. "You can be with someone for years, buy a house, raise a family. Then somewhere down the road, you find out he's on the down low or he wants out or – "

"I just don't want to see you get hurt," Angie interrupted. "I just hope you know what you're getting into is all."

"That's just it. I'm not as naïve as everyone thinks I am. I'm being very realistic. You know, you grow up watching all these Cinderella stories and they all have these happy ever after endings. But no one tells you that Cinderella really had a sequel, that in time she became the evil stepmother, that her Prince Charming died an alcoholic and left her to raise his dysfunctional kids by some trick across town."

"But Carmen, it's such a big step."

"It's a viscous cycle and I want off. You know, you first get here and you're the new girl on campus. The guys break their necks wanting to take you out. You spend all this time planning and getting ready for a date. The day comes and you don't have anything to talk about. And you and he both know he's really only after one thing. You succumb to pressure. After a while, you're no longer the new girl. The freshman meat wagon comes to town and all the guys want to do is sample all the new meat now. You push past your comfort zone, because what you won't do, someone else will. Before the date is even close to being over, he's already planning the next date with somebody else. One night stand or committed relationship. They all end the same. It's too much."

Carmen hadn't even scratched the surface. Being raised in church, she thought some of the men there were bad enough. She thought she had seen it all – infidelity, baby mama drama, lying, cheating, hypocrisy. But she had no idea how crazy it was in the real world. These guys had no restraints. They were straight out heathens. They ran trains, turned girls out, date raped, told their girlfriends who to screw next. The frats were known for trading their girlfriends to fellow frats faster than the stock market. Girls sold their bodies. She had seen her share of small town Christian girls get turned out by male and female alike.

Times were different. Love was just a notion from her parent's day. For her today was all that mattered, she'd let tomorrow worry about itself.

"And that's why you have to stand for something or continue to fall for all the B.S. they bring your way," Angie insisted. "Unless you're willing to hit rock bottom, you can't afford to play the game. Some things take patience. Even guys have to wake up and realize that the party won't last forever. Just like new girls come in, new guys come in too – with way better game. And when men decide it's time to settle down, that they can't keep up, who do they look for? Somebody who has stood their ground, who knows what they want, who has stability, somebody they can build a future with."

"That's what I've been trying to say! It's all politics. Thanks," Carmen said, as the waiter brought out their drinks.

"What are you saying? Are you settling?"

"Remember Iesha, my friend from back home?"

"I remember you mentioning her."

"We came up together. My mom and her mom were real cool. In fact, her house was the only house I was allowed to spend the night at because everything with both our moms was about church. Iesha and me both, we heard it all the time. I even heard it from her mom and she heard it from mine. Then we go to church and we'd catch it there. Iesha got to be just as bad. 'You can't wear this.' 'You can't do that.' Always checking me. Fast forward to prom night. Iesha gets pregnant. She turned right around and did the very thing she preached against."

"I'm still not following you."

"Iesha was too concerned with how it looked on the outside, to all those people around her. Deep down she was hoping that something would jump off between her and her boyfriend that night, that they'd get caught up. That way she could say it was an accident. That she didn't mean for it to happen when that's what she wanted all along." Carmen took a sip from her pink lemonade. "The difference between us. I owned up to mine. I lost my virginity the same night. Only I planned to, it didn't just happen. I took all the necessary precautions. Yeah, I still got hurt. Thought me and Mike would be together forever, but at least I didn't go into it blind. So now Iesha's at home raising a child, still living with her mom, praying that one day God will reunite her with her baby's father instead of being here at school with me like we had always planned. I stopped living in a fantasy world a long time ago. The bottom line is I'm not waiting on God to rain down manna from heaven. I'm securing my future."

"So basically what you're saying is you don't trust God."

"Why should I? Look at His track record. How many Christian women ever get to walk down the aisle? Statistically it doesn't happen enough."

"But aren't you going to the other extreme?"

"Meaning?"

"You've always said that women with educations have a shoe in when it comes to keeping a relationship. So it becomes all about accomplishments. You shelter yourself in your accomplishments, like they will guarantee you happiness. Like somehow your success will ward off all the other stuff that can go wrong."

"No."

"Carmen, yes you are. Do you hear yourself?"

Carmen sighed. "I'm just saying that my mistakes are my mistakes and no one else's. That I'm going to live my life and if I mess it up, it's on me. It won't be because of how someone else said it's supposed to work."

"But you don't have to experience every mistake, Carmen. Learn from somebody else's. Some things you just don't do. Some of these young girls that get here, they don't have any home training, but you do. You don't really have an excuse. I know you think your parents went to the extreme with church and all, but don't throw everything they taught you away because of it."

In a word Carmen considered her parents boring. They were too strict, too religious and out of touch with reality.

"Are you calling Todd a mistake?"

"I'm not calling him anything. I don't know him. I'm only asking you if you do."

Angie saw that Carmen was shutting down.

"Listen, just know I wouldn't be all up in your business if I didn't care. I'm only asking you to be honest with yourself. Not me. Not your mom. But yourself. Nothing more. Nothing less. And with that I'm done."

Angie had this same talk with others many times before. What Carmen was doing was nothing new. A few listened. Most didn't. She had learned to speak her peace and leave it at that.

"So what's going on with Diane? Has she decided what college she wants to go to?" Angie asked, moving on to the next.

CHAPTER 9

"**Why did you** start so late?" Todd asked as he joined Carmen in the kitchen, perusing the choices she had laid out for tonight's occasion.

"It's a dinner party. Nobody eats as soon as they walk through the door."

Todd sampled the spinach dip. "You obviously don't know these two," he said, squeezing Carmen in approval.

Tonight's menu consisted of chicken cordon bleu, wild rice, scalloped potatoes, garlic bread, a vegetable platter, spinach dip, and for dessert, apple cinnamon crepes served with caramel sauce.

Not even a minute later, the door bell rang.

"They're here," Todd said as he went to answer the door.

Doug walked in first. "Hey, man."

When Joy walked in, her eyes grew as big as a kid in a candy store. "Aww, sookie, sookie, now! Look at you! You struck a gold mine! Where she at?"

Carmen peeped from around the corner. "How's everybody?"

"Ah, she just a little thang, Todd. How you manage that?" Joy asked as she went to greet her.

"Hi, I'm Joy."

Carmen held out her hand. "I'm Carmen. Nice to meet you."

As Joy shook Carmen's hand, she rolled her eyes to Todd letting him know she wasn't buying it and if

Carmen wanted to play like she was all that, count her in too.

"And this is Doug," Joy said, suddenly putting on an air.

"Hey."

Doug wasn't helping Joy's case at all. He had been staring at Carmen, his mouth slightly open, since she rounded the corner. When he didn't stop drooling, Joy finally popped him on his head.

For a moment no one said anything.

"Well, make yourself at home. I'll be right out with the appetizers," Carmen said, breaking the silence.

"Yeah, ya have a seat," Todd said looking at Doug like he had lost his mind.

Joy and Doug followed Todd as Carmen finished putting the finishing touches on dinner.

"This is nice, Carmen," Joy said after being seated.

"Thanks."

"What style is this?"

"Eclectic."

"Lec – who?"

"Eclectic. It just means that none of the pieces really match."

"You can say that again," Joy mumbled under her breath.

When Joy informed Todd that she would be over for dinner, Todd thought about knocking her out cold, but she had too much dirt on him, so he halfheartedly complied. He warned her well in advance to behave, but Joy was going to be Joy.

"Why don't you give us a tour, Todd? You don't mind, do you, Carmen?" Joy asked before Todd could protest.

"Oh, go right ahead."

Joy took it all in as Todd led her around. Two bedroom. Plush carpet. High efficiency washer and dryer.

Ceramic tile. Ceiling fans. High end appliances. Jacuzzi tub.

Todd opened the door to the bathroom and closed it before they could step inside. He then opened the door to the master bedroom. When he tried to do the same, Joy pushed her way past him. Doug stepped inside too, but stayed at the door while Joy carried out her inspection. Todd pulled the door close.

"Why you got to be so trifling?" Todd demanded.

"Ain't nobody being trifling but you. You living like this and you can't pay me for all that time you stayed with me? Uh uhn. I ain't having it."

Joy stuffed her bra with Carmen's special occasional gold hoop earrings and cash she found in one of the dresser drawers.

"You happy now?"

"This don't even start to cover it."

As Joy headed to the closet to snoop there, Todd opened the bedroom door.

"You say something, Carmen?"

"I didn't say anything!" Carmen answered as Joy rushed out behind Doug.

As they returned to the living room, Carmen came out with appetizers.

"Ain't this nice. You all domesticated. So what you do for a living?" Joy asked, as she looked Carmen up and down.

"I work for the State Department of Education Training and Assessment Division."

"Doing what? Cooking or cleaning?"

Carmen wasn't sure if it was a joke. "No, I work as a curriculum specialist."

"A what?"

"It's just a fancy name for someone who helps decide what books and things schools and businesses will use for training."

"How did you manage to get into that?"

"I did a lot of volunteer work for the public school system my first two years. I think that's what got my foot in the door."

"Let me get this straight," Joy said. "You volunteered for two years and didn't get paid?"

"Yep. So now she does that and she goes to school," Todd said proudly.

"So you work for a school and you go to school. That's a lot of school!"

"What about you?" Carmen asked.

"Ain't that much school in the world!"

Carmen looked surprised.

"I mean, I'm done with school. I work as a Professional Assistant to the CEO."

"That sounds interesting. Where is this?"

"In his office."

Carmen was expecting Todd to have friends over from the job, maybe even from his college days – but these two – no way.

"So, Doug, how do you and Todd know each other?"

"We came up together." Carmen waited for him to elaborate. Doug then asked, "You got something to drink?"

When dinner was ready, Carmen did a final inspection. Todd joined her in the kitchen. He stood behind her and snuggled against her.

"It smells good. Have a seat. You've worked hard."

"You sure?"

"I got this," he assured her, giving her a smooch on her cheek.

Carmen took off her apron then joined her guests in the dining room, taking the seat across from Joy.

"I hope you not trying to poison me or nothing, like that, Todd!" Joy called out.

"Why would I do that?" Todd asked as he dug a booger out of his nose and hid it inside Joy's chicken cordon bleu.

Joy looked at Carmen. "Don't mind me. We joke like that."

After dessert, they returned to the living room.

"Do you stay in town?" Carmen asked Joy as she sat on the arm rest of the love seat next to Todd.

"Honey, I practically stay right up the street from you! In fact, I see you walk past my apartment all the time!"

Carmen wondered why Todd had never mentioned Joy to her.

Todd gave Joy a dirty look.

"Look at you two," Joy said as she cleared her throat. "So how long have you been engaged?" she asked, attempting to switch the subject after Todd frowned at her.

"A few months now," Carmen replied.

"Where's your ring?"

Carmen threw her arms around Todd's neck. "I got my man. That's good enough for me."

Carmen turned to peck Todd on his cheek, but he caught her lips and tongued her as Joy and Doug watched.

Once again the room grew silent. No one said anything for about the space of a minute.

Finally, Doug broke the silence. "You got something else to drink?"

Carmen smiled and returned to the kitchen in search of some hidden libations for Doug to suck down. She couldn't wait for this night to be over. He had already drunk two bottles of her best wine pretty much by himself. As Doug waited for her to return, he spotted the games to Todd's X-Box Kinect mixed in with the collection of DVDs.

"You didn't tell me you had a X-Box!"

Damn!

Reluctantly, Todd got up and opened the drawer to the entertainment center that hid the X-Box console from view.

"Hurry up, man!" Doug yelled as Todd loaded the boxing game.

Doug started laughing. "She looks like you, Joy, except her name is Pain."

By then, Carmen had come back with Doug's drink. It was painfully obvious that Todd had Joy in mind when he created his avatar's opponent. Joy scratched at the back of her head, embarrassed that everyone saw the resemblance. Doug then did that ignorant laugh. Carmen came this close to placing where she had heard it before. He was about to laugh again, but he stopped when he saw that Joy didn't appreciate it.

As Carmen tried to remember where she knew Doug from, Joy sank back on her love seat, lit up, closed her eyes and inhaled. Just that fast, it left her. *Cannabis. In my apartment.* It was not the first time she had been exposed to it, just never in her place. Doug reached over and Joy handed off to him. He took a few puffs. Carmen looked at Todd. These were his friends. He should be saying something. But then Doug passed it on to Todd. *So he's a recreational drug user. What other vices do I not know about?*

What a waste of time, Carmen thought as they had been at it for more than an hour. While she worried about the ventilation, they had gotten the munchies and devoured a bag of chips. She got up to go to the kitchen. Todd tapped her leg.

"Where you going?"

"To clean up."

"Stay and watch. I'll get it."

Carmen sat back down and watched as Todd and Doug took turns against each other, then Doug against Joy, recalling how differently Todd had behaved when she had company. Not long after, Doug slipped and just missed the glass cocktail table.

"Hey!" Todd shouted.

"That's enough," Joy finally said. "Whew. I'm tired. Let's go before you tear up something and they don't want us back."

Todd saw them both to the door.

"We got to do this again soon, Joy," Doug said as he followed Joy out.

"I don't know about that," Todd said. "Ya'll ain't got to go home but ya'll got to get the hell outta here!"

Laughing, Todd slammed the door behind them. Carmen wrapped her arms around his chest and squeezed him from behind thinking that tonight didn't have to be a total waste.

"You're high, aren't you?"

"Yep."

"Let me get you to bed," Carmen said playfully as she began to lead him towards the bedroom. She turned back when he didn't budge.

"I can make it. You just clean up this mess." He kissed her goodnight then left her to deal with the aftermath on her own.

CHAPTER 10

"You're home early," Carmen said as she dropped her things at the door.

She heard Todd in the kitchen running water when she came in. She looked around. The place was spotless. He had been cleaning religiously and from what she could see, he had done a pretty good job. Even the carpet looked cleaner than it had in a while. Todd emerged from around the corner to greet her.

"You are too cute," she said as Todd turned for her, entertaining her with a variety of poses as he modeled his apron, proving that he could make anything he wore look good.

He was being playful and carefree. She had never seen this side of him.

"What is that I smell?"

"Your favorite. And I ran your bath water."

"How sweet," she said, feeling that this déjà vu was inescapable as she began to relive this all too familiar scene once again.

"Take your time," Todd said as though he knew *I'll be right back* would be what she would say next.

Carmen smiled, but was fast becoming anxious as she wondered what surprise awaited her tonight.

When she returned from taking her bath, the food was on the table as before, but this time Todd had lit candles and R&B slow jams played softly in the backdrop.

Todd pulled Carmen's chair out for her then poured her a glass of wine.

"I like it when you get off early. You have the nicest surprises waiting for me," she said, hoping to no longer delay the suspense of whatever he had yet to share with her.

"Well, it'll be a lot more of this now that I no longer have a job to go to."

"Oh, baby. What happened?"

"They let me go. They said business just hasn't been good enough to justify keeping me. They decided to contract my services out instead."

"Didn't you see it coming?"

"Not this soon. The big thing in law now is these companies who specialize in research. They have bigger data bases than all my resources combined. Information is practically at their fingertips. They're fast becoming the drive thru of law offices around the world, especially with the economy the way it is."

"So what now? How are we supposed to make it with neither of us working?"

"That's where I don't want you to worry. I can draw unemployment to the max if I don't find something else. And if we have to, I always have my savings and pension. And if it would make you feel any better, if Mr. Shelton will take you back, you can go back to part time."

"Really?"

"Really."

"I was hoping you'd change your mind because I never told Mr. Shelton that I quit, only that I couldn't go full time. I couldn't bring myself to do it. Are you mad?"

"A woman's intuition. How can I be mad at that. And just so you feel good about it, I got you a little something."

Todd dropped to one knee as he pulled a princess cut two and a half karat diamond ring from his apron pocket, catching Carmen completely off guard. She gasped, elated that he cared enough about her to get her a ring.

"Carmen Daniels, will you marry me?"

Carmen couldn't stop shaking as Todd slid the ring onto her finger. Things from here on out were going to be different, she just knew it, she could feel it. She rose from her chair and threw both arms around Todd as he lifted her from her feet. "Yes, I'll marry you!"

* * *

"Engaged?" Her mother could not believe her ears.

"That's what I said, engaged," Carmen confirmed in her mature, everything is under control voice.

"To Todd? This man you've been seeing for only, what is it, two months?"

Carmen crosses her fingers over her heart. "Closer to four. I met him before I moved here."

Carmen held the phone away from her ear.

"I know you're a grown woman now! Lord knows that it's hard for me, but I do try to respect that! But this, Carmen! Baby girl, for your sake! Please back up before you step into something you couldn't get out of if you wanted to!"

"But we are taking it slow, Mama," Carmen assured her. "The wedding's not till next year, after I graduate."

Her mother sighed. "That's a little better. Are you pregnant?"

"Mama, of course not. I'm smarter than that. You should see my ring."

"So he did get you a ring. That's nice, but don't let that man think he owns you because you're wearing his ring."

"He's not like that at all, Mama. In fact, he wants me to go back to school full time so I can go on and finish."

"How are you supposed to do that and work full time too?"

Carmen took a deep breath. "Because he's taking care of us."

"Carmen, don't tell me that you let this man move in with you!"

"Well."

"How long ago was this?"

"A couple months ago now. . . . Mama, are you still there?"

Carmen's mother held the phone to her chest then finally returned it to her ear. "Have you quit your job yet?"

"We decided I'd stay at part time."

"Carmen. Listen to me real good. You keep your own bank account."

"I already have one."

"Then start one he doesn't know about. I don't care if it's only ten dollars a pay check, you save that religiously. Can you do that for me?" Carmen sensed an urgency in her mother's voice that hadn't been there before.

"Yeah, but - "

"No buts, Carmen," she said sternly.

Todd then appeared around the corner, and snuggled against Carmen, kissing her neck.

"What is it for?"

"Let's pray we never have to find out."

* * *

Fall classes were back full force and so was Carmen.

"Why are you getting in so late?" Todd asked the moment Carmen walked in. He had been sitting in the corner, waiting on her.

"I went to the library. I had to look up research material," she answered as she set her backpack on the dining room table. She flipped on the light then searched her backpack for her cell phone.

"I've been trying to call you."

Carmen barely looked at him. "I turned off the volume. I got caught up and forgot to turn it back on."

She then took her cell into the bedroom and didn't come back out. When Todd saw that Carmen hadn't come straight out, he followed her.

"Who are you talking to?"

Carmen covered the phone with her hand. "Angie. I'll be out in a minute."

"A minute is too long," Todd said as he stood in the doorway.

Carmen was tired and she was not in the mood. "Like I was saying, I think you should take it. They have good insurance, a solid retirement plan, and they have a reputation for – "

Todd snatched the phone out of Carmen's hand, closing it. "I said a minute is too long!"

"What has gotten into you?" Carmen asked as she looked up at him.

"This school thing is not working! It's consuming you!"

"That's what going full time does!"

"It's not just school! It's everything!"

"Why are you so hypersensitive? Are you like . . . bipolar?"

Todd slapped Carmen so hard that she tumbled across the bed and fell to the floor. He jumped across the bed after her.

"I got yo' hypersensitive!"

Carmen scurried back against the wall.

"Oh, you want some more?"

Todd balled up his fist. Carmen hid her face and screamed. Todd then rammed his fist into his hand as Carmen screamed again. For the longest, he just stood glaring down at her waiting for one wrong look, one bad move for it to be on again. Finally, he left the room. Carmen stayed in the corner, scared to move.

* * *

"Do you know I've been worried sick about you?" Angie said as she walked in Carmen's office.

"The call dropped. I didn't have time to call back," she said as she swiveled her chair to hide her bruise.

"You sure about that?" Angie asked.

Carmen wouldn't look at her. "We just had a stupid argument is all."

Angie paused for a moment then took a deep breath as she sat in the chair across from Carmen's desk. "Carmen, there's no easy wall to tell you this. Todd is not who he says he is."

The hairs on the back of her head stood straight up as she waited for Angie to explain herself.

"Eric Denton – the man my aunt used to date from Gallagher's. I called and talked with him. Todd Henry works there all right. Only he's about twenty years older and has a family and remembers running into another Todd Henry who was more than a little interested in learning all about his career. Todd doesn't have a law degree – at least not from State he doesn't."

When Carmen walked in, she heard Todd in the second bedroom, pumping weights, the metal click clacking against itself as he counted out repetitions. Quietly, she closed the door and looked around her apartment. It was filthy. Fall semester had barely been underway two weeks and the place looked like a tornado had ripped through it. Dirty dishes were piled in the sink. The dishwasher was full of dirty dishes. Todd's blender sat on the counter with banana and protein powder slime trapped beneath its blades.

Carmen crept into the bathroom careful not to alert Todd. She looked past the dirt rings that covered her porcelain fixtures and sat on the edge of the tub. She had no idea how to handle this situation. She wasn't even sure what purpose was served by coming home. Angie couldn't be right; she had to have her facts mixed up. Carmen was heavily in denial. As she dropped her face in her hand, she saw where Todd must have tried to hide mail in the bottom of her mesh garbage can. She took it out. Her eyes darted back and forth as she flipped through each page, two and three times, then once carefully. It was a bill – in her name, her credit card she reserved for emergencies. Carmen's heart beat a mile a minute. There were a ton of new expenditures, including charges for new furniture, some of the furniture unaccounted for, and a two and a half karat princess cut diamond ring.

Todd met Carmen as she was coming out of the bathroom.

"We need to talk."

"I left my book. I'm running late for class," she said, refusing to look at him.

"Baby, you don't know how sorry I am. I've been under so much stress and – "

"I need to get there on time, Todd."

As Carmen tried to walk past him, he pulled her close, saturating the entire side of her face in his sweat.

"You make me so crazy. Sometimes I feel like I'm losing you."

"For real, Todd. When I come back."

* * *

"Excuse me, but does Todd Henry live here?"

As soon as Mario heard Todd's name, he stepped outside. "Not any more. You know him?"

"That's what I'm trying to figure out."

Mario let down his guard when he discovered why Carmen had come knocking. In fact, he felt a bit sorry for her once he realized that she too had to be one of his many victims.

"If you don't know him, save yourself the trouble."

"Why?"

"Because he's a thief. A no good two bit hustler."

Carmen felt herself getting sick to her stomach as Mario confirmed her worse fears.

"I left him to watch my house and he stole all my good stuff. He ain't been back here or to work since."

Just thinking about it made him mad all over again. Mario himself had done his share of dirt. While some would say that it had come back on him, that he had finally reaped what he sowed, he couldn't disagree more. Serving three years up state, he had paid his debt to society. He had been out going on four years now and was determined to never go back. He had since built a life for himself. His situation was in no way ideal, but everything he owned, he earned it the old fashion way. He was proud of his accomplishments, able to sleep at night after a hard day's work, something he couldn't do before. He understood all too well what it was like to be down on his luck, dependent on the help of family and friends until he could get reestablished. It was what he had tried to do for Todd.

"Where did he work?"

"With me at Bobbie's Chicken 'N Ribs over on Helm."

The shock on Carmen's face let Mario know that she'd had all the revelations she could stomach for one night.

"Do me a favor. If you find out where he is, let me know."

CHAPTER 11

How on earth, *when, what the? Oh, Lord, what have I done?!* Her heart was beating so hard she thought it was going to break through her chest. Something was off kilter about him, she had felt it from the start. *And what if he, you know, I can't even say it – maybe he is a little bit – more or less . . . functionally retarded? This grown ass man picks his nose, for crying out loud! And come to think of it, I've never seen him read anything. And what if he can't read? Then talking on the phone, using big words, not all of them in context – probably just a bill collector on the other end. And what about?* She covered her mouth with both hands. *What if he has AIDS? What if I –*

She tried to trace her steps back to the moment she went wrong. It wasn't when he slapped her across the bed. It was before that. It wasn't when he disrespected her with her mother on the phone. It was even before that. It wasn't even when she let him move in. But it was when she crossed #3 off her list. She hadn't given herself time to heal from her last relationship.

Her issues with Vivian were deeper than money. Carmen and Derrick had been on again off again then one day it was over. He didn't call. He didn't stop by. She had feelings for him and although he cared for her as well, he wasn't ready to commit. Around April, he started coming back around. Nothing was official, but she knew it was leading somewhere.

Vivian was the type of jump off who got on Facebook and requested other females' male friends, even their exes, not because she knew them, but because she wanted other women to know she had it like that. She wanted to get under their skin. She was always in front of the camera. Posing half naked pictures, her ass all over the lens. Although Carmen and Vivian shared an apartment, Vivian and Derrick had never run into each other. One day Carmen was coming home and Derrick was leaving out. He didn't say a word. He didn't have to.

When she met Todd it wasn't so much that she was lonely as it was that she was vulnerable. That night Todd left without saying a word was all a mind game. She had fallen for one of the oldest tricks in the book. Her black Adonis was just that, Satan transformed into an angel of light, a counterfeit. She had never healed from the wound Derrick inflicted. Then Todd's rejection added to her insecurities. When he came back, he came with acceptance, he rescued her at a time she needed it the most.

* * *

When Carmen made it back, Todd was in the kitchen talking with Joy as she progged through her cabinets like some carnivorous scavenger on the hunt for road kill. From the time Carmen met her, she had become a nuisance. She spied on Carmen from her apartment, anxious for her to get on the bus so she could stop by and take her things. Pots. Pans. Tissue. Movies. Her vacuum. And really, who borrows wine?

Joy had gotten comfortable with her too fast. She was tall. Big boned. Boisterous. The type who went to stores, got out of line then expected to have her spot when she came back. She probably never thought twice about cussing out the elderly or beating on other people's kids. She was intrusive and overbearing. She probably peed standing up. At this point there was no sense in sugar coating it – Joy was ghetto, plain and simple, with a capital G, H, E, two T's, and four O's.

"Class let out early?" Todd asked.

"Yeah."

"Todd said I could get a plate. You don't mind, do you?" Joy asked. She was so preoccupied that she never even looked at Carmen.

"No. In fact, if you don't mind, I'm going to turn in early and let Todd keep you company," Carmen said, making Joy being there seem as if it was of no consequence.

"I'll be sure to bring your plate back," she promised, once again lying through her teeth.

With Joy raiding her refrigerator and Todd keeping watch, Carmen quickly searched for the keys to Todd's trunk. She checked several of his pants pockets before she finally found them tucked away in a jacket hanging near the door. When she unlocked the trunk, there were stacks of mail, credit cards, driver's licenses, even bills, none with his name on them, everything randomly tossed about. She fumbled through it, having no time to process who they belonged to or why they were in his possession. She was only looking for one name – his. But there were no accreditations, letters of reference, resumes, not one certificate or theses that suggested lawyer in the pile. She was close to the bottom when she found the check stub from Bobbie's Chicken 'N Ribs.

Just when Todd thought she had finished, Joy started a second plate.

"Why you looking like that? She said it was okay," Joy said in her defense.

When she had finally finished piling layer upon layer of leftovers, she searched for foil to wrap her plates.

"What ya doing next Monday?" she asked as she ripped off more foil than was needed.

"Get out, Joy. Now."

Carmen heard the front door slam. She tucked the check stub inside the back of her panties with her sweater covering the rest. She replaced his keys and was at the end of the bed pretending to hunt for her gown when Todd came in.

"What you looking for?"

"I was looking for my night gown," Carmen answered as she sorted through the clothes lying next to the bed.

"You didn't give me a kiss when you came in."

"You were busy talking with Joy. I didn't want to interrupt," she said as Todd moved closer.

"She's gone, so what's your excuse now?" he asked as he took Carmen by the hand.

Carmen stood to her feet as she faced this familiar stranger, a man she suddenly knew nothing about. Todd pulled her close. As his lips met hers, he ran his hand across her butt, then up her back. Carmen tried to move, but it was too late. Todd snatched the check stub from her clothing. The moment he realized what she had done, he grabbed her arm.

"You couldn't let well enough alone."

"Let me go. You're hurting me."

"I'm hurting you? I give you nothing but trust and this is how you repay me?"

"But you lied."

"I told you what you wanted to hear. Did you think some business type was really going to come to yo' rescue? Baby, stop dreaming. You can't do better than me."

"Let me go!" Carmen demanded as she squirmed, unable to break from his grip.

"So you can leave me?"

"I didn't say that."

Carmen managed to pull loose. As she glared at him, Todd casually walked to the door and locked it. He then took one of her belts off the door rack and folded it in half.

"Take off your clothes."

"No."

Todd popped Carmen's leg.

"Take off your clothes."

"No!"

Todd hit her several times indiscriminately.

"Do I have to tell you again?" he asked as he slapped the belt across his hand.

Carmen slowly pulled her sweater over her head then sat at the end of the bed to remove her shoes. She leaned back to unzip her jeans with Todd watching her every move. She tugged at her jeans until they lay on the floor.

"Don't stop there," Todd instructed, barely able to contain his excitement.

Carmen slid her panties on the floor then lay back.

Todd walked past her and began pulling her clothes from the closet.

"Get in the closet," Todd commanded as he stripped her belt from her robe.

"For what?"

"Don't make me ask you again!" he shouted.

Carmen begged him not to hurt her as she complied with his demand.

"Hands up! Grab the bar!"

"Todd, you know I love you," Carmen said as she placed both hands around the pole. "We can work this out."

"I know we can," Todd said as he tied her hands above her head. "But you've been a bad girl. What happens to bad girls?"

"I said I was sorry," Carmen cried.

"Too late for that," Todd said as his sweats dropped to the floor. He then parted her legs allowing the weight of her body to rest on his arms. Breathing obscenities, he sucked and nibbled her ear as he leaned into her, anchoring her back side against the wall. The more she begged him to stop, the more he behaved like a prisoner on furlough. Excited by her fear and disgust for him, he pushed and grunted until his legs shook violently. As he climaxed, he stumbled. Carmen fell as far as her bound arms would permit.

Semen flowed down Carmen's thighs as Todd pulled his sweats up. He then held a finger to Carmen's lips warning her to keep quiet. He then lifted her finger and snatched off her ring.

"If you pull this bar down, I'll make you eat it. Is that understood?"

Todd shut the closet door then left the room.

* * *

The sun shining through the blinds hurt Carmen's eyes when Todd finally opened the closet door.

"Open your mouth. Come on. I ain't got all day."

Todd fed Carmen a few bites of a frozen pastry he had heated in the microwave. As he untied her hands, she crumbled. Todd carried her over to the bed. Carmen's head slumped to her chest as she tried to sit upright.

"I'm late for work," Carmen said.

"How can you be late when you no longer work there?"

"But we need money."

"You ready to be a good girl?"

"Yeah."

Todd used Carmen's phone to call her job. He tried to hand her the phone, but her hands were weak and shaking and her circulation had not returned. Todd held the phone to her ear.

"Make it sound good."

"Hello. May I talk to Mr. Shelton?" Carmen asked after someone had finally answered. "Mr. Shelton. This is Carmen. I'm sorry I didn't call earlier, but I had a family emergency. . . . Yeah, it's serious. It's my mother." She began to cry. "You know I would do this the right way if I could, but I'm flying back home. . . . Yes, this is my resignation."

By now, Carmen was sobbing.

"I want you to know that I appreciate everything you did for me. Tell everyone I said goodbye."

Todd ended the call.

"You appreciate everything he did for you?" he asked, drawing his hand back.

Carmen flinched.

"Oh, baby," Todd said as he stroked Carmen's cheek, "If you would just do what I tell you. Keep people out of our business and we wouldn't have this problem."

"What do you want from me, Todd?"

" 'What do I want from you?' Do you know how good that sounds?" Todd turned Carmen's face towards him. "Let me be the man in this relationship. That's all I've ever wanted."

Todd walked to the end of the dresser and held up Carmen's accordion file for her to see.

"All your personal information – birth certificate, social security card, license – all that. I'm keeping it for you."

Todd threw her file in his trunk and locked it. He then walked back towards the bed and stood in front of Carmen. Her eyes were blood shot as she looked at him. He held her cell phone in front of her then snapped it in half.

"What about my mother?"

"What about her?"

Carmen couldn't stop crying.

"Relax. You show me you're ready to be a real woman and I'll let you talk to her . . . sometimes."

CHAPTER 12

Angie was on her way back to her car when Carmen answered the door. Angie could barely see her face when she peeked out.

"Carmen!" she said, sounding surprised as she turned around. "You're still here. When are you flying back?"

Carmen hesitated as she recalled the lie she'd told Mr. Shelton. Now that she was being held captive, she had more pressing issues to think about.

"I'm not. It wasn't as bad as I thought."

"How is your mother," Angie asked, as she got closer.

"I didn't want to say anything to Mr. Shelton, but my mother's fine. It's really Diane. She's getting out of control and Mama can't keep an eye on her and Alicia by herself. In fact, she thinks Diane is pregnant." Carmen was talking real fast.

"You were always a terrible liar," Angie said as she approached the sidewalk leading to Carmen's stoop. "Don't let this man ruin your life, Carmen."

Angie was just about to turn up the sidewalk when Todd pushed his way past Carmen, swinging the door wide open.

"From the day I met you, you struck me as the jealous type," Todd said as he stepped past the stoop with his arms folded. "This really isn't any of your business, Angie."

"Carmen can speak for herself!"

"Yeah, Angie. Just like she did with Vivian. I'm only going to tell you this once," he said pointing at her. "I'm not Vivian. Don't let me catch you around here again."

Angie looked towards the door. "Can't you see this man is crazy?"

Todd looked around briefly before stepping into the landscaping close to the front window. He scooped up a handful of gravel and began chunking it at Angie, piece by piece.

"Go inside now, Carmen!" he demanded.

Carmen dropped her head and did as he said. Angie stepped back as pieces of gravel struck her.

"This won't be the last time you hear from me, you ignorant bastard! I promise you that!"

Angie ran towards the end of the sidewalk as Todd threw the remaining gravel at her.

"Get a man of your own, Angie! It's nothing to see here people!" he shouted as several bystanders looked on. "You remember what I said!" he warned, looking towards Angie one last time. Todd then went inside and slammed the door.

* * *

The glass shattered as it slammed against the wall.
"I tried!"

"You didn't try hard enough! That's your money! You worked for that!"

"According to the letter, my job is still open. They said as long as they're willing to let me come back, I'm not eligible for unemployment. If I call Mr. Shelton – "

Todd bent over Carmen's chair and placed his lips directly to her ears. "You ain't calling nobody! You hear me?"

Carmen looked straight ahead and didn't answer. Todd then began pacing the floor.

"They denied you 'cause that nappy headed bitch Angie had to go running her damn mouth."

"I still have my scholarships. If you let me go back before I miss too many days, they'll give me the balance at the end of the semester."

Todd went into the second bedroom. He came back carrying a stack of books.

"Are these all your books?"

Carmen looked at the stack.

"Yeah."

"I'm selling them back to the bookstore."

He had already taken back her ring. Lord only knows what he had done with it.

"But, my scholarship – "

Todd got behind her again. "And no, you can't go back until I can trust you." He started walking away then came right back again. "And that might be never," he threw in as an afterthought.

Todd suddenly disappeared again. Carmen continued to look ahead of her, in a fog, baffled. Never in her wildest dreams did she see this coming. She had no idea of how to get out, where to even begin. So many times she wanted to hit the door and run like a mad woman, yelling bloody murder at the top of her lungs, but he was always somewhere close by. And if he caught her, what was he capable of? The thought of going back in the closest terrified her.

It had been several days now since Angie stopped by. Why hadn't she called the authorities? Or maybe she had and they told her exactly what Todd said they would, that their hands were tied, that they could do nothing.

"I'm letting you go back to work."

Carmen never saw him come back in.

"You want me to call Mr. Shelton?" she asked. For a split second, she came back to life.

"I never said where."

As Carmen looked into space, Todd walked behind her and dropped the employment section of the Sunday edition in front of her. She jumped. It took her a moment to figure out what she was looking at as she skimmed over it. She then saw the section that was circled in red.

"Telemarketer? Tuesday through Saturday? Second shift?"

"You got something against honest work?"

It was a good thing Todd couldn't see her face. It was at times like these when there were no words. She shook her head no.

"It says you can apply on line," Todd informed her.

So he can read.

"But you took my laptop."

"Oh, yeah. Don't get no funny ideas," he said, pointing at her as he left the room. "I'm watching you."

* * *

DAY 1 – October 2

Carmen finished brushing her teeth then glanced at Todd's reflection as she put her toothbrush back on the shelf. The way he was acting, she would have thought it was his first day on the job. Carmen then took ample amounts of gel, more than she normally used, and applied it to her edges. They resisted as she tried to smooth them into submission.

"Why is your hair sticking up like that?" Todd finally asked. "It's all over the floor."

"I need a touch up."

"How much is that?"

"Seventy-five," she said, hoping he would fall for it.

"To do it yourself?"

"About twelve."

"That's why you stay broke now. Tie a scarf around it. It's time to go."

"I need bus fare," Carmen reminded him.

"Relax. I got it covered."

Todd sat across from Carmen watching her the whole way there. Wondering just how much longer this charade could possibly go on, Carmen stared out the window and pictured herself making her escape. She looked for familiar landmarks, hoping that by some chance, today would be the day, even if she had to leave everything she owned behind.

They were headed in the direction of what used to be old downtown. Most the businesses in the area had long dried up. The strip mall bustled with customers during its heyday. Today only a few local retailers, a Cinnabon and mobile phone chains served as the main draw. Thru traffic was the primary reason old downtown hadn't turned into a ghost town by now.

Carmen was in deep thought when Todd asked her what she was looking at. She said nothing then put her head down for the rest of the ride.

Once they reached their destination, the building was just a few blocks down. Todd went in behind Carmen and sat with her in the empty reception area. Carmen kept her eyes fixed on her lunch bag just so Todd wouldn't ask her what she was looking at again.

Hardly five minutes had past when Sandy, her new supervisor, came out to greet her.

"Carmen Daniels? Come with me."

Carmen pulled her purse over her shoulder, then got up and followed her. She glanced back at Todd. Holding his index and middle fingers in a V, he pointed at his eyes first, then at Carmen's, letting her know that he was watching. He waited until he heard Sandy's door to her office shut, and then he finally dipped out.

"Have a seat," Sandy said as she sat at her desk. After Carmen was seated, she handed her a packet.

"The job is pretty straight forward. It's an hourly rate, but we do have a weekly quota that we expect you to meet. You have two times that if you fall below, you're given a verbal warning which also results in a write up. The third occurrence results in disciplinary action and or termination. Don't worry. You'll get a lot of rejections and angry people on the other end, but you'd be surprised at the number of people who in spite of the economy can still afford to go on vacation. We offer options including weekend packages they may not have otherwise considered."

Sandy had done this countless times before, but she still kept her eyes on her notes, making sure she covered every point.

"As an incentive, we do reward you for going above and beyond. As of now, you're on probation for 90 days. There's an automatic pay raise once you pass probation as well as benefit options if you so decide. It's all in your orientation material. Just remember that each time you miss a quota, it sets you back five work days. Once you make it through probation all previous occurrences are dropped. You start fresh and as a permanent employee you're given up to six occurrences per calendar year. You also have the option of transferring out. We have offices in Indiana and Virginia. The company will actually reward you with $500 to help you relocate, which I think is a pretty good gesture on their part. All they ask in return is that you sign on with them for an additional six months once you get there."

It was like a spark of hope reignited inside her.

"90 days and I can start all over?"

Sandy glanced at her. "You plan on relocating?"

"I just meant that making probation – it's like a new start."

Carmen quickly reasoned that at this point, it was unwise to let anyone know of her newfound plan to move away.

Sandy made a copy of Carmen's driver's license, on loan from Todd, then walked her towards the end of the hallway.

"This is a job with high turnover. We currently only have two permanent employees. We try to maintain a relaxed atmosphere, but tension can get quite high, especially towards the end of the week when everyone's scrambling to make quota. But don't let that bother you. Everyone's really nice once you get to know them."

They quickly reached the end of the hall. The telemarketers' office was on the opposite side of the hallway, down the hall from Sandy's office. The room was spacious, yet only eight tightly compacted cubicles took up the area. The abundance of exposed cable cords and telephone wires suggested that not much thought had gone into planning the layout. Rosalind was at the printer when they walked in.

"Rosalind, this is Carmen."

"Nice to meet you," Rosalind said.

"She's permanent and so is . . ."

"She went to the bathroom," Rosalind informed her.

"And that's Brandy in the corner."

Brandy peeped around her cubicle holding her phone to her ear. She waved and gave Carmen a big smile.

Sandy then pointed to the cluster of cubicles in the middle of the room where the outer walls were barely waist high.

"Just raise your hand! This is Chris, Jordan, Estelle, Charity," she said as she pointed to each of them.

"You'll be sitting there", she said pointing towards the back of the office. "If you have any questions, everybody's real good with helping each other. Take your time and get familiar with the material before you make your first call. And welcome aboard."

Carmen thanked her and started to head for her desk.

"Oh, there you are. And Carmen, there's one last person for you to meet."

When Carmen turned around, her face dropped.

"This is Joy."

"Why didn't you tell me you were trying to get in here?" Joy asked with that same air she tried to pull on her that night when Carmen first met her.

"But you said you worked – "

"I could of put in a good word for you!" Joy interrupted.

Sandy smiled. "So you two know each other. There you go. Already beginning to feel like home."

CHAPTER 13

"Brandy, what did I tell you about clicking that pen?"

Brandy looked up as if she had just been given a pop quiz. She swiveled her chair and looked at Joy. "What did you tell me about my pen, Joy?"

Joy still had her back to her. "I told you that if you didn't stop clicking that pen, you would have to move."

Brandy frowned. "I don't remember you saying that."

"Well, I said it. Don't take this the wrong way, but you're switching desks with the new girl."

"Are you serious?"

Joy stood up and began placing the few items that Brandy kept on her desk in Brandy's arms. She then placed Brandy's box of tissues on top of her small pile.

"Come on before the new girl gets comfortable," Joy said as she nudged her towards the opening of their cubicles.

It finally registered that Joy was serious even though she had been clicking that same retractable pen for as long as she'd been there. Brandy burst into tears. "But I like sitting with you, Joy!"

Joy directed Brandy towards Carmen's desk at the back of the room. "Girl, you're barely ten feet away."

"But Joy," she said, sobbing with her arms full.

Joy handed Brandy one of her tissues. "You can always come and visit. Are we still cool?"

Brandy shook her head yes.

Joy then held out her hand. "Keys please."

Brandy set her belongings on the end of Carmen's desk then pulled her desk keys from her pocket. Joy then waited for Carmen to collect her things.

"How's it going?" Sandy asked after coming back to check on Carmen after a few hours.

"I'm getting a feel for it."

"Good. Fill these out and get them back to me. Payroll needs them by Wednesday."

* * *

I can do this, she told herself as she hung up the phone and finished documenting her first sale of the night.

It wasn't the same as having an office to herself, but other than the phone, she didn't have to interact with as many people as she had on some of her previous jobs. It hurt her to think that she had given up a state job for this. Her own office was nearly half the size of this one. Her favorite wall, subway tile, gave her the sense of being in a pub rather than on a job. It was covered in posters of all the places she hoped to one day visit.

This space was tiny, but she had no plans on being here past 90 days so it really didn't matter. Besides, being in a cubicle helped her feel less accessible, which was how she preferred it. The way she saw it, any time she spent away from Todd was time well spent. She would spend the night if they let her.

She took out a piece of paper and started a list of the bare essentials she would need to get back on her feet. Unless Todd robbed her blind and disappeared before she got home, she would be forced to start all over again. First month. Deposit. Transportation. New phone. Utilities. Household basics. Food. Two change of clothes. Personal items.

90 days, Carmen thought to herself. She took out the calendar that was in her packet and counted back. It had been almost 90 days since Todd had tricked his way into her life. It would take another 90 days to get him out. She then counted 90 days from today's date. It put her at the end of December. The timing was perfect. It would be just enough time to get out of Dodge and allow her to enroll in winter classes. She didn't know which university she would transfer to in Indiana yet, she'd have to check it out. But if all her course work was transferrable, even after losing the entire semester, she could possibly still graduate by the end of summer.

But how do I pay for it without taking out a loan?

To date, she had not borrowed one red cent to pay for her education and she would really prefer to keep it that way. Her parents made sure that most of the money she scrimped and saved throughout her teenage years was tucked away for her education and if they had their way, she would have gone to community college her first two years. In retrospect, she wished she would have listened.

"So Carmen, how long have you known Todd?"

Carmen flipped her calendar and paper over, not sure how long Joy had been standing over her.

"A little while now," Carmen answered as she turned in her chair so that she could see her.

"You must really be in love with him."

"You two seem to be really good friends," Carmen said purposely deflecting Joy's comment.

"Same ol' crazy Todd. We've been hanging together since high school."

"Where was this?"

"It was here. You should know that."

Carmen hunched her shoulders. "We talk about so much. I forgot."

"You need an interoffice envelop?"

"Yeah."

Without warning, Joy picked up Carmen's payroll forms and placed them in the envelope for her.

"I'm headed that way," Joy said as she sprang to her feet. "I'll take it for you."

Carmen let it go. She waited until Joy had left the room. She then peered around her cubicle. "Excuse me. How do they feel about us using the computers for personal stuff?"

"You sit across from Joy and you haven't figured it out yet?" Estelle asked sarcastically.

"But is it company policy?" Carmen directed at Estelle. Estelle ignored her. Estelle was in her late 50's, grouchy, and was only there because she had to be. When Estelle didn't answer, Rosalind did.

"As long as you meet your quota, they don't care if you surf the net all day. Just never ever make any personal long distance calls on their phones."

* * *

"We break anywhere from 6:30 to 7:30. Come on," Joy said, ready for dinner.

"I prefer to wait."

Joy pulled Carmen by her arm. "Come on. Keep me company."

When they got in the break room, Carmen checked the refrigerator. Rosalind saw that she was searching for something.

"Something wrong?" she asked.

"I could have sworn I left my bag right here."

"It probably got covered. That contraction sees a lot of activity," Rosalind responded.

Carmen thoroughly checked a second time. "No, it's gone." She then looked in the garbage. Her plastic container and the paper bag she carried it in were both in the trash. "Somebody stole my food!"

"That is low down," Joy said as she removed her frozen entrée from the microwave.

"It was probably an honest mistake," Rosalind said. "Around here you have to put your name on it or its subject to become public property. You like chicken salad?"

"Yeah, but I'll be fine," Carmen said, not wanting to impose, especially since she had just met her.

"I won't take no for an answer. Grab a plate and come on."

Carmen looked around for a brief moment before spotting the paper plates on top of the refrigerator. Rosalind gave Carmen half of her sandwich then went to the vending machine as Joy and Carmen were seated.

"I wouldn't eat that if I was you," Joy whispered. "I hear she got roaches real bad. And be careful what you tell her. She keeps up a bunch of confusion."

Rosalind came back from the vending machine with two bags of chips and sat across from Carmen. "You pay for one and two falls out – imagine that."

"Thank you."

"So Carmen, is it? You from around here?"

"No, I just thought this is a good place to go to school," she said, remembering how Todd warned her not to talk to anyone and not knowing if Joy might run back to him and repeat everything she said.

"That's a smart choice. So which one do you attend?"

Joy nudged Carmen. "I'm not enrolled yet. I need to save money first."

"Well, you won't get rich here, but if you set your mind to it, you can do it," Rosalind encouraged her.

Charity came around the corner looking in the break room. "Joy, Sandy wants to see you in her office."

"Tell her I'm eating."

"She said now."

Hesitantly, Joy got up and headed to Sandy's office while Carmen picked away at her chips. Rosalind waited until Joy had rounded the corner.

"And for the record, I don't have roaches. I bought that chicken salad fresh from the deli yesterday."

Carmen looked at her half of the sandwich. It really did look appetizing. She finally took a bite and smiled. "This is good."

When Joy came back, Carmen and Rosalind were laughing as they left the break room together. Carmen returned to her cubicle. Joy grabbed her dinner and followed. As Carmen went to sit down, she saw a sticky note on her computer to call Todd. Her heart nearly stopped. She took a deep breath before she picked up the phone.

"Hello. . . . It's going pretty good. . . . No. . . . I said no."

"Is that Todd?" Joy asked, turning towards Carmen.

Carmen shook her head.

"Tell him I said hi."

"Joy said tell you hi. . . . Yeah, that Joy. . . . She's sitting right across from me. . . . Because I didn't know she worked here." Carmen then turned towards Joy. "Todd wants to know if I can ride home with you."

"Of course," she said, as she ate her dinner.

"She said yeah. . . . I love you too. . . . I said I love you too." Carmen closed her eyes and shook her head. "I said, I love you too!" she said, loud enough to be heard by all her coworkers. Carmen hung up the phone and dropped her head in embarrassment.

* * *

"When I was asking you what Todd was like in school, what did you mean by same ol' crazy Todd?"

Carmen was seated in the passenger seat of Joy's 2007 Chevy Sonic as they returned to Windy Creek Apartments.

"Just same ol' crazy Todd, why?"

"Nothing. It's just if . . . since I'm going to marry him, I don't want any surprises," Carmen said, scratching her head, hoping that Joy didn't catch her slip up.

Joy took her eyes off the road for a brief second. "Has Todd done something to you?"

"No, I was just asking," Carmen said, as she pulled her wind whipped hair from her lips. Carmen feared that she had said too much.

"Todd is my boy and all that, but between me and you, he can be a little over possessive. Don't take this the wrong way, but if I was you, I'd put some money aside and if you ever decide you want out, take the money and run."

"That bad?" Carmen asked.

"Girl, that's nothing I wouldn't tell my pastor's wife," Joy assured her. "I just know break ups can get sloppy. I believe in saving yourself the trouble of trying to sort through the little stuff and just go on with life. No sense wasting valuable time, right?"

"Right."

"So what did you and Ros talk about at break?"

And just when she thought she might have found an ally in Joy. Carmen looked at her. Joy was aware that Carmen was suspicious of her being so personal, but pretended not to notice.

"I was just joking about her having roaches. Everybody who knows me knows I play a lot. But on the real – don't be telling everybody your business."

"I don't do that any way."

"Good for you."

Joy blew the horn when she pulled in front of Carmen's apartment.

Why on earth did she do that? Carmen thought to herself.

Carmen expected for Todd to be outside waiting on her or to rush straight out. As Joy pulled off, Carmen took her time walking towards the stoop not wanting to alert Joy that something was wrong. Carmen watched as Joy's break lights came on at the bend then off as she turned the corner. If she was going to bolt, now was the time. But she couldn't. Todd wouldn't let it be this easy. It had to be a trick.

Carmen slowly unlocked the door and went inside. All the furniture was gone. She then ran into her bedroom. Empty. Todd was gone. He was really gone. She got excited. She had gotten her life back. *The locks, I have got to change my locks. And then* - As Carmen went to leave the bedroom, Todd stepped in front of her. Her heart sank.

"What's going on, Todd?"

"We moved."

"Why?"

"Because I thought it was in our best interest, that's why."

Carmen didn't get it.

"I didn't break our lease if that's what you're worried about. We're just around the corner. Come on."

CHAPTER 14

DAY 12 – October 13

"What happened to you?" Joy asked when Carmen came in.

"I was running late. Sorry if you had to wait."

"I'm talking about that chia pet you got on your head!"

"I'm overdue for a touch up."

"I know money is tight, but girl! You 'bout to sprout branches and birds and shit!"

Carmen sat down and tried to ignore the unnecessary attention Joy brought her way.

As much as you hide behind wigs and weaves, you probably don't even have any hair your damn self, you overgrown Sasquatch.

Every time Carmen dropped her guard, thinking Joy wasn't quite as bad as she thought her to be, Joy turned right around and reminded her of just why she really couldn't stand her to begin with. And she had the nerve to be talking about money being tight when she obviously couldn't afford to buy her own stuff. She still had a lot of her best cookware and hadn't bought her vacuum back either. And what about all that gas money she had the nerve to charge her when she practically lived next door?

Carmen pulled her scarf from her purse and tied it around her edges. Today she was officially three weeks overdue for a touch up. Her hair was dry, brittle, and the split ends were creeping back at an alarming rate. Her scalp was itching nonstop, making it hard for her to concentrate on her work. If she could get a touch up soon, she could still salvage it. She'd have to cut it a few inches just to make it not look so uneven though. But even after that, it still wouldn't all be the same length. At least no one else would ever know.

Yeah, won't that be fitting? she thought to herself. All the cover up going on in her life and no one, not even Angie, had any idea how extensive the damage actually was.

A few hours passed and Carmen was returning to her desk.

"What is this?" she asked Joy.

"It's mail. Duh."

"Why is it on my desk?"

"Because around here we take turns delivering interoffice mail. Most of it's for the law office upstairs."

"How do I know whose desk is whose?" Carmen asked, as she thumbed through the mail.

Joy still had her back to her.

"Because anybody in that type of profession has a name plate on their desk. You're college educated and you don't know that?" she asked, rolling her neck, purposely getting loud.

Rosalind took note.

That's twice in one day now. What is up with her? Carmen wondered as she left to deliver the mail.

Dinner time finally rolled around. Carmen left out right after Joy had come back. She was hungry, but not hungry enough to have dinner with Joy. Carmen wasn't gone but a few minutes when she was forced to return to her cubicle.

"I thought you were taking your break," Joy commented.

"That's the second time somebody stole my dinner."

Brandy overheard her. "Don't feel bad. I had five dollars in my drawer yesterday. It's not there now."

"It ain't nothing I hate worse than a thief," Joy chimed in. "I told you to keep your drawer locked, Brandy."

* * *

"Yes, the upgrade is well worth it," Carmen said to a potential customer. "You heard me right. It includes an extra night, dinner for two at one of the participating restaurants and an upgrade to a five star suite. All that for an additional $159. . . . You decided to go with the upgrade? That's great."

Joy mocked her when she said *that's great*. Carmen thought she heard her do it, but didn't have time to think about it.

"So if you have your credit card handy, we can get started."

* * *

"Ma'am. That's not what I told you," Joy said with a snap in her voice. "We have a script that we read and I read it to you word per word. . . . No. I said that if you chose the Vegas package or the Miami package, that they have limo service from the airport. Denver doesn't have that," she said nastily. "That package comes with car rentals only."

Joy held the phone away from her ear as the person on the other end complained.

"I need to check that out. Let me put you on hold."

The customer protested, but Joy did it anyway. Joy then waited for Carmen to return from the bathroom. As soon as Carmen sat down, she transferred the call to her desk.

"Dreams Come True Travel. . . . I'm sorry ma'am. I don't know who put you on hold, but let me pull up the account."

Right before Carmen had a chance to figure out whose sale it was, Joy got up and left. Carmen stood up and covered the phone. "Joy! Joy!"

Joy kept right on walking.

* * *

Joy was busy surfing the net when Brandy came back with checks.

"Look what I got," Brandy said, waving checks like they were hundred dollar bills.

Brandy distributed checks beginning at the back of the room and made it to Carmen and Joy's cubicles last.

"And after two weeks of busting your butt, congratulations," she said as she handed Carmen her check.

"Thanks." Carmen smiled as she opened her envelope, but frowned as soon as she saw the amount. She quickly checked the figures. "My bonus is missing. Isn't that supposed to be separate?"

"It should be," Joy answered as she watched her.

Carmen was counting on the bonuses to break free from Todd. This was not acceptable.

"Is Sandy in her office?"

"She left for the night already," Joy answered.

"No, she's still here," Brandy said.

Carmen got up to find Sandy before she ducked out.

"What did she tell you?" Joy asked when Carmen came back.

"She said I didn't do enough to get a bonus. I worked my ass off for that $25."

"They got me too when I first started. What you do from here on out is make a copy of all your sheets before you turn them in," Rosalind advised her.

* * *

Joy did not know when to shut up. She talked Carmen's ear off all the way home when she could plainly see that Carmen was not in the mood for conversation. When Joy pulled in front of Carmen's apartment, Todd was waiting outside. He motioned for Joy to get out. Joy rolled her window down.

"What?"

"Come and see!"

Joy parked and got out. She followed Todd into the kitchen. A box perm was on the counter.

"I want you to perm Carmen's hair for me."

Carmen's mouth fell open.

"Now?" Joy asked.

"You see how it's falling out."

"I just got off work. Don't you see how late it is?"

Carmen picked up the box and read it. "But this is extra strength. I only use gentle."

Joy took the box from her. "You ever use this brand, Carmen?"

"No."

"Trust me," Joy said, "this company don't know shit about extra strength."

"So when can you do it, Joy?" Todd wanted to know.

"I'll come by tomorrow."

"But I know how to do my own perms," Carmen spoke up. "I do them all the time."

"With the new growth you got? Girl, you better take help while you can get it!" Joy exclaimed. She then looked at Carmen's face. "Relax. I've been doing perms for other people for as long as I can remember. In fact, I do mine too. You got my gas money?" she asked, looking directly at Carmen.

"Do you see a bank open this late?" Todd countered.

"Don't play with me," Joy warned him.

"You get that after you do her perm," Todd informed her. "That way you got to come back."

* * *

When Joy came through the door, Carmen was all set to go. She had on an old loose T-shirt and had applied petroleum jelly to her scalp and edges. In case Joy really didn't know what she was doing, Carmen had even applied it across her forehead, brows, ears and down her neck. She had divided her hair into four sections all of which she had taken the time to detangle just in case Joy didn't know how to do that either. She had applied conditioner over the old perm in case Joy for some dumb reason decided those sections needed perming too. She had her timer, her towel, extra gloves and a comb. She was ready.

"Where she at?" Joy asked, when she came in.

Todd was busy playing his Kinect. "She's in the kitchen. What took you so long?"

"You ain't the only one that likes to sleep in."

Carmen was already seated at the sink.

"Look at you," Joy said as she opened the box. "You did this much, you might as well of done it yourself."

"Just trying to save time."

Joy mixed the activator into the relaxer.

"Wait a second," Carmen said when she saw how quickly Joy had mixed it. "Let me see that."

"Why?"

"Because it's going on her hair!" Todd shouted from the living room.

Joy held the container for Carmen to see.

"It's too many lumps."

"What lumps?" Joy asked as though she didn't see any.

"Hand it here." Carmen took the container and mixed it to her satisfaction, then gave it back to Joy.

"It ain't even that serious," Joy said as she began smoothing it on Carmen's nape.

Carmen ducked. "Uh, uhn – start in the middle and don't let it touch my scalp."

"I know what I'm doing."

"Then do what she said!" Todd shouted again.

Joy smacked her lips and followed Carmen's instruction while Carmen set the timer. She moved quickly as she covered Carmen's head with the creamy substance. Carmen ducked several times when Joy applied too much pressure. Joy backed off quickly, as she was tired of hearing Todd's mouth. She then took off her gloves and joined Todd in the living room. Twelve minutes had hardly gone by when Carmen's eyes began to water.

"Joy, this is starting to burn!"

"I just put it on you!"

"But still!"

"You want it straight, don't you?"

"Yeah, but – "

"You need at least 30 minutes then!"

Carmen sat quietly for the next few minutes. Straight or not, it was time to wash it out. "Joy! My head is on fire! Wash it out! Now!"

Joy rushed into the kitchen and looked in the box. "Can you believe it? They didn't put any neutralizer in here. I got some at my place. I'll be right back."

Joy hurried out while Carmen tried to wait it out. She tried counting to a hundred but didn't make it past eighteen. Carmen was pacing the floor when Todd came in to check on her.

"Girl, sit down!"

"My head is on fire!"

Carmen then ran in the bathroom and sprayed oil sheen over her entire head. The oil sheen only worked for a moment before she jumped up again. Carmen grabbed the box to the relaxer and out fell the neutralizer. Todd grabbed it.

"Didn't she tell you to wait?"

"Todd! Please! It's burning!"

Carmen snatched it out of Todd's hand. She barely covered her fingertips with the gloves then adjusted the water with her head under it. She heaped on the neutralizer, washing the relaxer out as fast as possible.

When Joy came back Carmen was in the bathroom.

"Where she at?"

Carmen stepped out with a handful of hair. Patches of her hair were gone.

"I'll be damned. That was super strength."

CHAPTER 15

"That wig looks good on you," Joy said when Carmen got there.

Carmen knew Joy was trying to be funny, she didn't even care. All she knew was Joy was the cause of her hair loss. It was because of her that she now had chemical burns and blisters that were still forming. Carmen counted five places so far, the size of quarters where her hair was missing. It was actually gone! Nothing! And practically everywhere else, it had come out in clumps. She couldn't touch her scalp, she couldn't sleep on it. Even air and water made it burn.

As dumb as Sasquatch tried to play, she had to know that caustic lye would eat up her scalp. That's why she kept trying to press it into her brain every chance she got. And it was mighty funny how when she came back with the neutralizer, that she didn't walk past the door, didn't make any attempt to inspect Carmen's hair for herself. She just dropped it and ran knowing that Todd was about to snatch her up, otherwise she wouldn't have left her car running.

Carmen sat down and carefully lifted that mangy animal fur Joy called a wig, that Todd insisted she wear, off her head, and flung it in the corner. She then loosely tied a scarf around her edges.

"I found another wig you might like," Joy said after witnessing how she treated the other one.

Carmen intentionally ignored her. Even Todd was so mad that he didn't want her riding in with Joy that afternoon. Yet Joy didn't know when to stop. She made several remarks to Carmen and when that didn't illicit a response, she asked her a direct question. Still, Carmen said nothing. Joy finally left to deliver interoffice mail. Carmen took out her bare essentials checklist and began to revise it.

New phone. Scratch that. Two change of clothes. No longer necessary – all I need is the clothes on my back.

She then took her calendar off the wall and marked off Saturday through Monday which put her three days closer to her goal, but not close enough. Seventy five days left. Seventy five days too many. She entered the name of her bank in her browser and signed into the online account she had established after the talk she had with her mother. The account that Todd knew nothing about. The screen displayed showing her balance. $80 wasn't a lot, but if it wasn't for her mother, it would be $80 she didn't have.

Tears began to stream down her face. Suddenly she wished she could hear her voice, talk to her, tell her what was going on. Tell her how she was right about so many things, about allowing a man to move in with her, about being too easy to trust, and how she was right about those ridiculously harsh chemicals she didn't need to put in her beautiful hair. Todd allowed Carmen to talk with her, but he was always standing guard. Her mother sensed something was wrong as Carmen always got quiet when she was troubled. Her mother would then remind her, even tell her stories of the strong women in their family. She would remind Carmen of how far she had come and encourage her to put her trust in God. But what stuck with her was when she talked to her father. He didn't say much. All he said was that it was time for her to come home.

"Tough day?" Rosalind asked as she stepped into her cubicle. "Anything you want to talk about?"

Carmen logged out of her account and faced her.

"Only if I thought it would do some good."

"Joy can be overbearing. Don't be scared to stand up to her. She's just un medio, excesivamente nina juguetona en un woman' cuerpode s," Rosalind said, calling her a mean, overly playful girl in a woman's body.

Carmen responded in Spanish saying that Joy was loud at that.

"So you know Spanish!"

Rosalind was impressed.

"I've been learning it as my second language."

"I knew there was more to you. With Spanish as a second language, you have a world of opportunity. Don't get stuck in this place."

"Has anyone ever transferred out before?" Carmen asked. She would hate for all this time to have passed only to find out she was wasting her time.

"In fact, just this spring."

"Do they really pay to help relocate?"

"That they do. Betina, she transferred to Virginia. She thought she'd never see the day. If you decide at some point that's what you want to do, make sure you don't let Sandy know. She's a good supervisor, but she takes transfers personally," Rosalind said, confirming what Carmen had picked up about Sandy during her orientation.

"Why is that?"

"It's hard to find dedicated workers in this job. And it makes her pay check fatter. You stay encouraged."

When Carmen walked into the break room for dinner, she almost walked into Joy as Joy was turning the corner. Joy was boldly eating her dinner.

"That's my dinner! And those are my earrings!"

It was the first time Carmen had actually looked at Joy all day.

"Not any more."

"What is wrong with you?" Carmen demanded.

"I'm not the one walking around acting all funny. I told you I was sorry, like accidents don't happen."

"That neutralizer was in the box the whole time and you knew it!"

Joy snatched Carmen's wig off. "Get smart with me again!"

Carmen had always been nonconfrontational, always shied away from conflict. Everything in her told her to hit Joy with all her might, just do it. She'd lose no doubt, but at least she would have stood up for herself. But Carmen couldn't do it.

"What I ever do to you, Joy?"

"This ain't about you. It's about Todd."

"Todd?"

Joy took another bite of Carmen's dinner.

"That's right, Todd," she said as she crunched away. "That nigger stayed with me three months – didn't pay no rent, ate all my damn food, didn't clean nothing – just trifling. So since ya'll together now – that man and wife become one shit – "

"We're not even married!"

"It don't matter. He told me you would pay me back."

"I don't know anything about your arrangement!"

Joy poked Carmen in her shoulder. "That's why I'm telling you myself. In fact, you owe me too."

"For what?"

"Who do you think helped Todd pick out your furniture? He gave me the earrings as payment."

Carmen's mouth fell open.

"So this is what you gonna do. Go to Sandy and tell her you made a mistake."

"But you stole my sale – and my earrings! Those earrings were not cheap!"

Joy went on as though Carmen had said nothing. "And tell her we worked on it together and you forgot that you decided to give that one to me. And make it sound good."

Joy balanced her plate in one hand and slapped the wig back on Carmen's head with the other, then had the audacity to pat it twice before returning to her cubicle.

* * *

When it was time to go, Todd was waiting in the reception area. Carmen lost her momentum the moment she saw him. Joy walked right past him and told him to come on. He got in front with Joy while Carmen hesitantly climbed in back.

Joy started the ignition and lowered all four windows as far as they would go. She backed out, rolled past the speed bump at the entrance and cranked up the sound system. Street lights illuminated Todd as he fired up a joint. He took several pulls then passed it to Joy. Joy took a long drag then gave it back. Her eyes teary, Carmen caught the brunt of the late night air laced with hemp. She sat quietly, fixed on the earrings Joy now boldly claimed as her own.

It was all so clear now. Todd and Joy were both the devil and each was the others minion. Joy was Todd's insurance policy to keep her from leaving him while she was on the job. And whatever Joy knew of Todd's past was the only assurance she needed to make sure he paid her back.

Carmen peered at Todd. His forearm grazed the car's exterior as he held the joint out the window in case he had to drop it at a moment's notice. Carmen was convinced that Todd had done this before. That this was a pattern. He used women, left them destitute, then moved on like a virus from one host cell to the next.

After Joy pulled in front of Carmen's apartment, Todd told Carmen to go inside.

Carmen peered through a crack in the curtain as they had a heated exchange. When Todd finally got out it was obvious they had called a truce. Carmen backed away from the window. She decided it was best to tell him what Joy had revealed to her since by now she was sure he already knew.

"What else did she tell you?" Todd asked after Carmen had spilled her guts.

"That's it."

"You sure about that?" Todd asked as he studied Carmen's face to determine if she was lying.

"Yeah."

"With as much gas money as she charges me, ain't that a bitch?"

"And she keeps stealing my dinner," Carmen said. Her posture was that of a child telling on a bully at the playground.

"I got something for that," Todd said. "Since you dumb enough to let her take it, no more dinner for you," he said as he poked her in her chest.

"But – "

"In fact, all you get is one meal a day. Stupid bitch."

* * *

DAY 16 – October 17

Joy left her cubicle for dinner and came back a few minutes later with a major attitude.

113

"I bet not see you eating nothing," she whispered in Carmen's ear as she stood over her. "Brandy! Hold up!" Joy shouted as she spotted Brandy heading out for dinner.

Joy unlocked her desk and grabbed her wallet and ran after Brandy. Carmen looked over her shoulder. Joy's desk was wide open. But before any thought could solidify, Joy was back.

"Thought I was leaving, didn't you?" Joy asked, as she returned to lock it.

Carmen sat in the break room after everyone else had taken their breaks. Joy came out and checked to make sure she wasn't eating. Carmen pretended to be reading a magazine. After Joy left, Carmen pulled out change she had saved and bought peanuts from the vending machine. She then ripped a credit card application insert from the Woman's Day and tucked it under her blouse.

CHAPTER 16

Carmen expected Joy to already be at her desk when she got there, but Joy was even later than she. Carmen may as well have been invisible as Joy had no flippant remarks for her, in fact, she barely made eye contact. She booted her computer and right away got on the phone, only not the company phone. She hit speed dial and waited for voice mail.

"Don't play with me! Pick up! When I see you, I *promise* you gone be sorry! I swear you got the wrong one! You punk ass bitch! You don't know who you messing with!" she screamed at the top of her lungs.

Joy hung up and dialed again. This time she got through.

"Who the hell is she, Doug? . . . You screwing her? . . . You done really fucked up!"

Oooh, he must have said yes.

Carmen had to hang up in the middle of a call because of her tirade. Joy could care less that her coworkers had to put customers on hold due to her loud mouth.

"I'm beatin' yo' ass and I'm beating his too!" Joy shouted.

Apparently Doug had handed over the phone to his new friend.

"You skank ho! When I – "

Her cell phone suddenly died.

"Ain't this 'bout a bitch," she said, throwing her phone back in her purse.

Joy was huffing mad, tapping her desk, looking about wildly. It had to be the sex, Carmen thought to herself because Doug was about as shiftless as they come. By then, Carmen had picked up the phone and made another call just so it wouldn't be so obvious that she had been listening, gloating in Joy's pain. Joy turned around, looked at her, grabbed her purse and marched out, but just as fast, she came back.

For the rest of the week, that was pretty much how things went. Joy was so consumed with Doug leaving her that she didn't have the time of day for Carmen. Although Carmen appreciated the reprieve, it was the one time she would have loved to have been in Joy's shoes. She hoped and prayed that while she was busy working, that Todd was putting his time to good use, and was in search of his next Carmen. With the way he had been acting lately, it might not be long before he was out of her life once and for all.

Carmen ran her fingers under her scarf and touched her scalp. All of her burns had finally scarred over. Todd hated natural hair and he hated short hair. He told her that her hair was the only thing she had going for her. Since it had fallen out, Todd found her less appealing which resulted in the less time she spent on her back being his sex slave.

* * *

Todd was sitting at the dining table with Carmen's laptop when she came in. She never knew what to expect any more.

"You want to go back to school?"

Carmen hoped he wasn't playing with her. "Yeah."

"What's your financial aid password?" he asked, blindsiding her once again.

"I don't remember."

"Don't make me get up. You will be sorry."

She had never acknowledged how ugly Todd was before now. His muscles were all he had going for him. Without them, there was nothing special about him. She watched him as he dug for gold, his fingers all over her keyboard. And this was what she had allowed to come so close to corrupting her gene pool.

As Todd scooted back in his chair to get up, Carmen forked it over. She wanted to cry. She knew where he was going with this. Besides the password to her secret bank account, it was the only other password Todd didn't have in his possession – until now.

* * *

DAY 33 – November 3

"You were doing so well, Carmen. What happened?" Sandy asked.

Carmen shrugged without looking at her.

"You slipped a week. Consider this your verbal. Be careful," she advised her, then turned towards Joy. "Outstanding job, Joy."

"Thank you," Joy answered as she continued surfing the net.

In spite of Carmen locking her sales in her drawer, Joy was finding a way to steal them. Her only reason for not telling Todd was because she didn't want him to turn it on her, find some other basic necessity to deprive her of. Carmen's optimism was seeping out of her like a slow leak

117

in a tire, her hopes of ridding herself of Todd and his pit bull dissipating with each passing day.

Todd had absolutely destroyed her credit. He had used her main credit card to pay November's rent, but yesterday when he tried to buy groceries, both her main card and her emergency card were declined. Utilities were due, yet he managed to keep his cell phone and find money for protein powder that he consumed like it was going out of style. His recreational weed consumption – more a daily routine now. She was hoping, praying they would get evicted. That way he'd have to wake up and realize there was nothing more she could possibly do for him. But now that he had taken it upon himself to apply for financial aid on her behalf, he wasn't going any place any time soon.

Carmen unlocked her drawer and took out her checklist. She looked over her shoulder at Joy. Sasquatch was busy playing online solitaire. But it didn't mean anything. Carmen put her arm on her desk and leaned over her paper as she revised it yet again.

Utilities. I'll deal with those when the time comes. Scratch. Household basics. Who cares? Scratch. Personal items. With as hungry as I am? Double scratch.

All that remained of her list was first month's rent, security deposit, transportation and food.

* * *

"Joy said you got wrote up today."

"I can't make people buy what they don't want!" Carmen cried out. She hadn't been home for hardly five seconds and he was at it again.

"That's bull shit! You're trying to get fired!" Todd shouted as he stood over her. "You know what you're

118

problem is?" he asked as he pushed her with his chest. "You got it too good."

He then turned away, leaving Carmen standing alone. She closed her eyes. When she thought it was safe, she let her purse slide to the floor and went to the bathroom. As she sat on the toilet, she noticed her discharge. It had never been this thick. Normally it thinned out the closer she got to her period. She rolled it between her fingers. It had a yellow ting and the odor was stronger than she ever remembered it to be.

Todd burst through the door. Carmen quickly stood to her feet, pulling her panties and pants up in one sweeping motion, she then flushed. As she reached for the faucet, Todd blocked her. Carmen ran to the tub and turned the hot and cold water on full blast. When she stuck her hands under the high pressure flow, Todd bent over her and twisted the inside of her upper arm. She shrank back in pain.

"Since you can't seem to keep your mind focused on work, no more clean water for you!"

Carmen sat on the floor next to the tub, holding her arm. Todd was breaking her down. She couldn't think any more. He had finally gotten in her head space and she couldn't win. She couldn't win.

I'm dying Lord, I'm dying! Get me out of this! I can't take it! Lord, please . . . whatever it takes, just get me out!

* * *

DAY 37 – NOVEMBER 7

She covered her mouth as she read the screen. Chlamydia would explain why her period had suddenly become irregular, the yellow discharge, and even why she thought she had been pregnant. And the painful sex, suddenly she wasn't sure if it was real or all in her head. Whatever she had, Todd had infected her from jump start. She scrolled to the bottom of the page and looked at pictures. After only three, she couldn't take any more. It made her skin crawl and her insides hurt.

Carmen never believed that her partners' sexual history became her sexual history, that whoever they slept with, she slept with to. In her mind she viewed condoms as a barrier to her partners' past. Only God knew what kind of history Todd had exposed her to.

How could I be so stupid? What is wrong with me?

She hated herself. She had been so caught up in fitting this magazine image of women who were respected for what they had and what they did, rather than for who they really were.

Any woman with any amount of self respect would not have allowed Todd to get as far as he had. She should have called the law office, checked the gaps in his stories. She should never have allowed him to move in without seeing his bank statements. At the very least, she should have never allowed that bastard to lay one hand on her when he showed up at her apartment without a condom.

CHAPTER 17

DAY 47 – November 17

Carmen was in the food line behind Joy. Joy sparingly filled Carmen's plate, but she heaped loads of food on her own. It was the potluck before Thanksgiving. Sasquatch was leading Carmen around like some pitiful creature in a sideshow circus, not caring at all about how their coworkers gave them sideway glances.

After the potluck had officially ended, Carmen took the initiative to go back for leftovers. She filled her plate with remnants of side dishes and took the last drumstick. When she closed the refrigerator door, Joy was standing behind her. Carmen tried to go around her, but Joy placed her in a headlock and snatched her drumstick. Carmen's wig tumbled to the floor. Carmen struggled but made sure she didn't let go of her plate. Rosalind just happened to be coming back for leftovers herself. It looked like some bad apocalyptic scene where the people had turned on each other. When Joy saw her, she let go. Rosalind didn't know what to think, didn't know what to say. Winded, Joy picked up Carmen's wig and threw it at her before she walked off with her drumstick. Carmen followed without saying a word.

When Rosalind went back in the office she purposely walked past their cubicles. Carmen was wolfing her food down as Joy reached over and snatched one of her sales from her desk. Rosalind waited until Carmen was alone.

"How long has Joy been taking your sales?"

Carmen bowed her head in embarrassment. "Since I've been here."

"You want her to stop?"

Carmen nodded.

"Did you know we have a separate listing for our Spanish speaking population? I'll talk to Sandy and remind her that you're bilingual."

"I never put it on my application," Carmen said, finally looking at Rosalind.

"No difference. Now let's see Joy steal those."

* * *

DAY 53 – NOVEMBER 23

"Thank you for choosing our company and have a great day," Carmen said in Spanish as she closed another sale. Only two hours in and she already had a total of three. Somehow it gave her the strength she needed to fight. In spite of her verbal, she was over half way there, closer to the end of this nightmare than the beginning. After she picked up her printout, she returned to her cubicle. She glanced at Joy. Joy was struggling. The more rejections she got, the more desperate she sounded. Carmen locked her sale in her desk. As she got up to deliver the interoffice mail, she couldn't help but wonder what the repercussions would be this time.

* * *

The moment Carmen set foot inside, Todd slung her across the room. She fell. Her knees caught the bulk of his wrath, but she still tried to crawl away. Before she got far, Todd snatched her up by her legs. She screamed.

The more she pleaded for him to stop, the more violent he became. Repeatedly, he rammed his fist in her thigh. In desperation, she latched onto the cushion but only managed to pull it off the couch. She wiggled until he lost his grip and she crashed to the floor. As she tried to crawl again, Todd stomped her back. She curled up in a fetal position and covered her face. Todd kicked her again.

"The only Spanish that comes out of your mouth better be over that damn phone!"

In a fit of rage, he dug his fingers into her scalp, but her hair was much too short to grip. Fresh blood instantly filled the scratches. He then snatched her off the floor, carried her into the dining area and flung her like a rag doll at the furniture. Her limp body plummeted to the floor.

When Carmen came to, she was laying in her bed wearing Todd's favorite silk negligee. She tried to raise up, but she could only roll onto her side. She then heard Todd come back. She closed her eyes as he closed the door. He climbed into bed and lay next to her. He then slid his arms around her waist and cradled her against him. She felt his heart beating as he softly kissed the back of her head.

"You ever leave me, and I will kill you."

* * *

DAY 54 – NOVEMBER 24

Rosalind stopped by Carmen's desk after Joy had gone. Carmen winced when she touched her back. Rosalind could tell something was wrong from the time Carmen walked in. Rosalind grabbed the interoffice mail and directed Carmen to follow her to the law offices on the second floor.

"Did Joy do this?" Rosalind demanded as she looked at the bruises on Carmen's back.

"My fiancé. He pays her to watch me." Tears streamed down Carmen's face as she revealed the secret she had kept bottled up for far too long.

"I don't understand."

"He owes her money. He's too lazy to work."

"Si. Do you have family here? Children?"

"No."

"Then do yourself a favor. Get on whatever will take you out of here the fastest – just get out. Do you hear me? Just go!"

"But I don't have the money. He's ruined my credit. My checks go straight into direct deposit and he controls that."

"Nothing, huh?"

"Not enough to start over."

"And if you wait to get the money, that chance may never come."

"Yeah, but I only have until January the eighth before I make probation. Then I can finally move."

"It doesn't matter. Listen. I was in the same boat you are. Before I moved here, I lived in Burt, this small town in Iowa where my husband is this big shot carpenter. He has his license, so he's the man. Only thing, he can never get the work he thinks he deserves. So what does he do? He takes it out on me. Tell me when I say something that doesn't sound familiar. He started arguments I didn't know I was in, he didn't want me talking to my family or friends, he called me names, he made me feel like I was wrong if I disagreed with him about even the dumbest things. Then he would throw things. He'd walk out and come back when he felt like I was ready to submit."

Rosalind closed her eyes and cupped her hands together, holding them over her mouth. She needed a moment to pull herself together.

"He would push, tell me how to dress, how to wear my hair, accuse me of cheating. Want to know where I was, what I was doing even when I was at home with him. Then that dumb stuff I never agreed with anyway, it became law in my house. The pushing turned to slaps and finally one day - he hit me. Yeah, he'd tell me how crazy I made him and he only did it because he cared so much. He got to where he would disrespect me in front of my daughter to the point she would do it to. My Maria was only five and calling me bitch. But I know she only said what she heard him say. He has a sister. She wasn't able to have children. She wouldn't help. She only wanted my Maria. So I saved change. A penny here. A dime there – for four years I did this. I had $139 when he found it. That night he beat me so bad. He put me in the trunk and drove me to the woods and left me to die. But I wasn't surprised," Rosalind said, shaking her head. "The month before I found an insurance policy he had on me, only I had never signed for it. But that didn't do it for me. No. It took him beating me to within an inch of my life for me to finally wake up."

"What happened to Maria?" Carmen asked, totally horrified by her story, especially the similarities to her own.

"I went back home. Not two hours later, I had his sister to come and get us. I gave her my Maria." Tears flowed down her cheeks. "If I stayed, he'd kill me and she would get her anyway. Right? Listen to me Carmen. *You've already got it better than most! There is no one keeping you here! You should walk out that door right now and not look back!*"

Carmen sobbed uncontrollably. "Don't you think I've thought about it every time I've walked past?"

"Then what's stopping you?"

"I don't know."

Rosalind put her hand on Carmen's arm. She knew her pain. Her fears. She then took a deep breath.

"Let's get this delivered before Joy comes looking for you," Rosalind finally said.

But it didn't really make any difference how long they took as Joy had been outside the office, eavesdropping on their entire conversation.

CHAPTER 18

"I must have called a hundred people today. Not one person showed interest. Uugh!" Carmen exclaimed to Rosalind when she came over to check on her.

"Let me see that list."

Rosalind thumbed through it.

"Did you tell Sandy you plan to transfer?"

"No."

"Well, this is her shit list. These numbers have already been called."

Carmen and Rosalind both looked at Joy's empty chair. Carmen's bonuses were still being rolled into direct deposit although she had gone to Sandy about it twice now and requested that the company cut her paper checks. With Joy no longer able to steal her sales, paper checks were crucial to her escape, now more than ever. It made Carmen nervous that Sandy had been so slow to resolve it. Todd was looking for her student loan to be approved any day.

Carmen took a deep breath, closed her eyes, leaned back in her chair, and blew out slowly. Deep breath in. Exhale out. She then took the interoffice mail and headed to Sandy's office to ask her about it once again. When she walked past, Sandy wasn't there. She then headed towards the elevator. On her way, she thumbed through the mail. *Mail for me?* She had totally forgotten about the credit card application she had submitted using the company's address. As she stepped off the elevator, she felt the envelope. There was plastic inside. She took another deep breath and opened it. Credit limit. $250.

When Carmen got back to her cubicle, Joy was there. Carmen played it cool and waited for Joy to leave before she unlocked her drawer and placed her credit card inside. She looked at her checklist again. Only four items remained: First month. Deposit. Transportation. Food. Another 38 days and it would all be over.

DAY 65 – DECEMBER 5

Rosalind hadn't been to work this week. Carmen asked Sandy if she had called in sick, but Sandy said she hadn't heard from her. Carmen was worried, especially since she had no way of getting in touch with her. She marked another day off her calendar. 34 days and counting.

Even with bonuses, she came up short on rent. She would have to pay a late fee at the end of the week. Todd had her call the utility company to make arrangements. Because she was already over 30 days late, they would only accept full payment. Not having lights only made her situation feel that much more intense. She and Todd didn't talk as it was and not having any background noise in the apartment made it even harder for her to be invisible. Nights were especially long and cold. Todd made her cover her head when he screwed her from behind. She feared he was going to take the money situation out on her, but for some strange reason, he was taking his aggravation out on his weights instead. It was disconcerting as she had no way of knowing what he was thinking. She wondered if he was finally done with her and if he was just waiting on her student loan so he could do her a favor and get the hell out.

DAY 66 – DECEMBER 6

Before it was time to go, Sandy stopped in to make an announcement.

"Where's Joy?"

"In the bathroom," one of the new girls answered.

"I need everyone's benefit enrollment form, whether you plan to participate or not. Tasha, Joy, Keith, I have yours. Everyone else – you have until the end of the week to get them back. Everyone that's on the phone, please finish your calls. I have something important to tell you."

Sandy waited for Joy to return. By then everyone who was on a call had finished.

"For your information, Rosalind isn't coming back."

Carmen jumped on her feet and stepped outside her cubicle.

"Apparently, she was living at a women's shelter and amazingly her husband found the location. Needless to say, he hurt her pretty bad. She came out of her coma, and she's stable. For those of you who would like to visit, she's in Brookfield. Let's remember to keep her in our prayers."

Carmen lost it. Joy stood and pat her shoulder. Carmen shrugged her off and ran into the bathroom. She dropped to the floor and cried her eyes out. How much more real did this have to be before she finally got it? She was in an abusive relationship. *Wake up, Carmen! Wake up!* Why on God's green earth was she still there? Did she need a trip to the emergency room? A near life experience to see that her life was in danger?

While Joy was on the phone, Carmen looked online at her secret account. She scrolled to the balance. It was a negative $48. She panicked. Immediately she called her bank. She gave them the information they asked for, whispering in as low a voice as possible. While they were accessing her account, Joy got up to go to the bathroom.

"Nonsufficient funds! I never made a withdrawal from that account! . . . You have got to be kidding!"

She was told that as long as she had an overdraft from any bank that was tied into their system, they had a right to pull funds from any existing account she had in her name.

Carmen got off the phone and unlocked her desk. Her credit card and petty cash, all of $11.37, was missing.

"Somebody's been in my desk!" Carmen shouted as she stepped out of her cubicle.

"Did you give your key to anyone?" Brandy asked.

Carmen held up her key. "No! It's right here!"

"Where's the back up key?"

"What back up?"

"Everyone gets two keys to their desk."

Carmen marched into Sandy's office and sat down uninvited.

"Why am I still on direct deposit?"

Sandy pulled out Carmen's file.

"According to our records, you never submitted a change."

"I've brought it to you twice now."

Sandy handed her another form. Carmen filled it out on the spot and handed it back to Sandy.

"Is something wrong, Carmen?"

"Did you ever stop to think that, I don't know, take somebody like me, that I just possibly might want to transfer out because I'm in a situation so similar to Rosalind's?"

Sandy took a good long look at Carmen.

"This is your verbal."

She ripped it in half. Tears rolled down Carmen's face.

"Thank you," she said in a barely audible voice.

I'll make sure that transfer money gets directly in your hands."

* * *

As Carmen sat in front of the computer, still shaken by Sandy's news, all she could hear were her mother's words, *you're too nice*. It wouldn't stop playing in her head. Of all things, why this and why now? When it wouldn't go away, she typed NICE in the search engine. WANTON and DISSOLUTE were the first two definitions she found on merriam-webster.com. According to them, the use of both terms was obsolete. She clicked on WANTON first. She was surprised to see UNDISCIPLINED as a definition. She then clicked on DISSOLUTE. She was even more surprised when she found that it meant lacking restraint and that it pointed to promiscuous sex as an example.

What exactly was her mother saying all these years? She then thought about something else her mother had said for as far back as she could remember: Nice is not a fruit of the Spirit.

Carmen then went to biblegateway.com on the browser and did a search for the word nice using the King James version, the only version of the Bible her mother trusted. Not only was nice not a fruit of the Spirit, it wasn't in the entire Bible – not one single time.

Carmen was perplexed? What was it her mother had been trying to get through her thick head?

She next looked at another definition: RETICENT. It meant inclined to be silent or uncommunicative in speech. It didn't take any stretch of the imagination to see how it applied to her situation. She then went back and looked at the origin of the word nice. It meant SILLY. Carmen didn't need a dictionary to know that silly was a character trait she didn't want identified with her.

She then went back to biblegateway.com and looked up the word silly. It came back with three results. The last one got her attention.

Second Timothy 3:6 – For of this sort are they which creep into houses, and lead captive silly women laden with sins, led away with divers lusts.

A light bulb went off. Nice was not a strength, it was a character defect. It was a doormat for people with ill intent. Nice was why everyone else's feelings were more valuable than her own. It was why people took from her with no intentions of giving back. Nice was just another word for sucker. It was why she had allowed people to dump on her what they would never tolerant from anyone else. Nice was why the users forgot about her when times were good, but the moment they found themselves in a bind, they came looking for her. Some even had the nerves to say God put her on their hearts, making her their only option. It made her the first resort for what they could do their damn selves. Nice never allowed her the luxury of telling people where to get off. After years of being nice, her only reward – a smile and a compliment in return.

Carmen was getting heated as she thought about how she had been used by Todd and Joy and all the people before them. She thought about how she would spend hours studying while others partied and how some of those same ones would casually whisper to her in class asking her to lean to the side so they could copy her answers. And what did she do? She let them do it. She asked nothing in return for sticking her neck out, for jeopardizing her own grades just to accommodate their spur of the moment selfish requests. Smart people would have at least turned it into a business opportunity. Would have made a profit, asked for something in return. And why did she do it? Because that's what nice people do. Nice people allowed other people to come in their homes and destroy everything they built, take everything they worked for.

Carmen was so mad at herself that she could bite bullets. She wasn't born into money, she just knew how to work what she had. Nice was why she had lost her job, had an STD, was not in school now, and was shacking up with some good for nothing bum. It was why she was hungry, and dirty, and didn't have any money – and why she didn't have any hair.

Carmen took out her phone book and checked the number before dialing. As she waited to get through, she unlocked her drawer, pulled out her bare essentials list and ripped it into shreds.

"May I speak with Evelyn?"

Her palms became sweaty as Carmen waited for Evelyn to come to the phone.

"Evelyn?"

"Yes."

Carmen had rehearsed this conversation in her mind countless times before, but everything she planned to say suddenly went out the window. She took a quick breath.

"Hi, this is Carmen Daniels."

"I haven't seen you in a month of Sundays! What can I do you for?"

Carmen suddenly felt this adrenaline rush come out of nowhere.

"After the way you butchered me, you can't be serious."

"Then why the hell are you calling me?"

"Because I wanted to let you know you had no right to do me the way you did."

"And you wait two years to tell me this shit!"

"Well, it can't be that insignificant, because after two years, you know exactly what I'm referring to. I don't know if you whacking my hair off somehow made you feel better about yourself, or maybe you were just jealous."

"Girl, please."

"If *your* problem was with *your* length, *you* should have taken that up with *your* mother and *your* father."

"What *you* should have done was come in here and talk to me woman to woman, especially about some old shit like that!" Evelyn shouted on the other end. "If you were standing here right now, I'd slap the taste out of your mouth."

"Trust me, if I could tell you face to face, I would. And you know, I would expect you to resort to violence because you're just evil like that. You pick on people you feel will let you get away with it. You cut my hair down to nothing because that's how you viewed me, as some weakling you could walk all over."

"But Carmen, really. What purpose does this serve? If you think you're making me feel bad – "

"No, this is so that I can feel better. I have lost more nights of sleep because of what you and other people have done to me while you go on like nothing ever happened. I'm telling you this now because I refuse to spend another minute of my life carrying this around with me. So I'm leaving this where it should have always been – with you. So if you choose to run from your conscience, I honestly really don't care. And if I were you, I'd be careful who I mess with. They may never say a word, but God knows . . . trust me, He knows."

CHAPTER 19

As soon as Joy pulled up to the apartment, Carmen noticed that the lights were back on. She feared the worse. Her money had come in and Todd was already squandering any hopes she had of a future away. Carmen went in. Todd was playing his Kinect.

"I got your favorite, you want it?" he asked in his all too familiar manner of having his back to her.

Carmen looked towards the dining area. Todd had gone to Sanford's Roadside Grille. Even with as hungry as she was, her first instinct was to say no. But saying no to Todd was asking for a fight.

"Yeah, thank you," she said, trying hard to sound appreciative.

"Go ahead, wash your hands. In fact, after you eat, I'll run your bath."

Carmen felt sick in the pit of her stomach, like an inmate on death row, preparing to eat her last meal. He was up to something. This would be strike three. Maybe he was planning to drown her. Say she fell asleep in the tub. Carmen deliberately ate slowly. Each bite went down like rocks. All she could think of was Rosalind and how she had warned her to get out while she could, but she was still here. There was no good reason why.

After she got off the phone with Evelyn, she felt alive, like she was taking back her life. Everything in her told her not to stop there. Just walk out the door and don't look back. Don't think about it. Don't analyze it. Just go. But like Lot's wife, she looked back.

By the time she finished dinner, Todd had her bath water ready. She got up and looked at him. He was seated on the floor, still playing his game. When she got in the bathroom, she quietly locked the door in spite of Todd's warning to never lock it again. If he was going to kill her, she wasn't about to make it easy. She undressed then checked the water before stepping in. Everything seemed fine. After soaking for a few minutes and Todd not trying to break down the door, it finally occurred to her why Todd was being so nice.

If student loans were anything like grants, the financial aid office would not release the funds without her going to the school and verifying that the money belonged to her. He needed her to look presentable. He didn't want to give the school a reason to think anything was wrong.

* * *

DAY 67 – DECEMBER 7

Carmen slept hard that night, especially after she came to the conclusion that Todd wasn't going to hurt her, at least not just yet. He had not come to bed. He had probably fallen asleep in front of his game, catching up for lost time now that the electric was back on. She got up and looked in the living room just to make sure. She was right. She went to the bathroom, then tiptoed into the dining area and got the roll she had left over from last night's dinner. She then returned to her room, careful not to wake him. She wanted to get up, but she knew better. If she woke him, he'd want to know what she was doing, so she climbed back in bed, ate her roll, and just lie there.

Only a few days ago, going back home to live with her parents was out of the question, but things had changed and she couldn't wait to get back. Even if Sandy did cut her a paper check, she needed her license in order to cash it. Without her license, she couldn't hop on a flight or get on the next bus out. Todd had told her a while back that he had taken it out of his trunk and put it somewhere she'd never find it. She hated the thought of him getting his hands on her money. And there was no guarantee that he'd take the money and leave. In fact, it might cause him to do just the opposite. What if he never left? Her eyelids grew heavy as she resigned herself to her fate.

She had not long dozed off, when she heard the doorbell.

She listened as Todd answered the door. When he didn't say anything, she assumed someone had the wrong apartment. She listened a few seconds more. Once she was certain no one was there, she closed her eyes and sighed. Todd would be coming in now that he was up.

Just as she anticipated, the knob turned and the bedroom door dragged across the carpet. It was time to get up and get dressed so Todd could escort her to the college before she had to be at work.

The door shut and there was a thud at the end of the mattress. One shoe hit the floor, then the other. Unless he planned on letting her take a shower, why was he doing this now? And why did he lock the door?

As the heavy impression lifted from the mattress, her body slid across the sheets towards the end of the bed. It wasn't Todd's hands. She opened her eyes. Doug was standing there. She rolled and dive bombed to the floor. She stood up quickly and screamed for Todd as she backed away from the bed.

"Girl, stop screaming. Who you think let me in here?" Doug said as though nothing was wrong.

"You're lying! Todd! Todd!" Carmen screamed at the top of her lungs.

There was a procession of taps on the door.

"Shut her up before somebody calls the cops!" Todd shouted from the other side.

"I told you. Todd let me in," Doug said as he held out his hand for Carmen to stop screaming. "Who you think paid your rent and your electric? It wasn't you and we both know it wasn't Todd."

Carmen was beside herself with fear. Her heart had never beat so hard in her life. She felt violated, like he had already raped her. Her feet froze to the floor. There were only two ways out – across the bed or past Doug.

Doug lifted his shirt over his head, swirled it around as if in a strip tease and threw it on the carpet. The front of his sweatpants stood at attention. He then smiled at Carmen and beckoned her towards him.

"Girl, you know you want this, get yo' fine ass over here and give big daddy some of that."

"No!"

"However you want to do this, it's fine with me," Doug said as he leaned slightly, ready for the chase.

Carmen made a mad dash across the bed, but Doug grabbed her before she could get across and slammed her on the mattress. She clung to the sheets as Doug dragged her towards him. Tears covered her face as she pleaded for him not to touch her. He held her down with one hand on her back. She scrambled to get free but he was so strong. He then looked behind him, searched around, found a scarf on the dresser and tied her hands behind her. He lifted her nightgown as he stood with her legs on either side of him.

"Girl, look at all this ass," he said as he grabbed her butt and squeezed, running both hands along her thighs.

Carmen had sudden recall. She remembered the day she stepped off the bus, the day she glanced at him and rolled her eyes. Right before she rounded the corner, one last time from her periphery, she caught a glimpse of him – and his friend.

"Don't do this," she begged, but he kept stroking her then he felt to see if she was wet. He promised he was going to take his time and do it right.

When he switched hands on her back, she knew it was only so that he could take off his other pants leg. He then flipped her onto her side.

He was butt naked, no condom, his thick penis looked like a huge turd as it extended past his enormous belly. He reached for the Vaseline that was on the dresser, and with one hand he uncapped it, scooped out an ample amount and slathered it on. Carmen scooted back on the bed, trying to get away from him but Doug held onto her, letting her scoot back until she was where he wanted her. He then climbed on top of her.

"Don't you have a sister, a daughter? How would you feel if somebody did this to them?"

Doug had just positioned her legs over his arms. He was only a moment away from penetrating her, when he stopped cold. He held her legs suspended for what felt like a life time as his conscience decided her fate.

"I only got brothers," he finally said, then licked her face.

Doug grunted and groaned as he plowed into her. He would look at her and start all over. His sweat made a sploshing sound as he pushed back and forth. When she stiffened her body like cardboard, he threatened anal sex. She loosened up and Doug had his way. His sheer size and strength stretched her inside and out, only adding to her discomfort and pain. Her legs were gapped farther apart than she was accustomed to. Her arms hurt. She could no longer feel her hands. After what seemed forever and a day, he lifted his torso, leaned to the side, and uttered obscenities as he climaxed, giving it everything he had left. He then pulled out and ejaculated next to her.

He looked down at her before he got up, like he wasn't satisfied yet. She was scared to move. Finally he climbed off the bed and got dressed. When he untied her hands, she moved to the other side of the bed while he sat on the opposite side and put his shoes back on. She didn't look at him and he didn't look at her. He just got up and left and shut the door behind him.

She sat on the side of the bed staring past the closet while he and Todd muttered something in the other room. It was only about a minute later when she heard Todd slam the front door. She looked right through him when he came and stood in front of her. He stared her down for the longest time. Finally, he grabbed her by her tiny afro and jerked her head up, forcing her to look at him.

"Don't think I didn't see how you two looked at each other. You been wanting to fuck him and you finally got your chance. Slut," he said, looking down on her in disgust.

Todd pressed her face into his crotch. "The only thing you good for now is sucking dick."

Carmen fought and kicked violently. Todd reached back and slapped her. She lay on the bed and covered her cheek as she looked back at him with nothing but hate in her eyes. Todd slid his thumbs down the sides of his sweats, but then reconsidered. Somehow he already knew. What Lorena did with a knife she would try with her teeth.

"Get dressed," he finally said, bringing the stare down to an end. "It's time to go to work."

* * *

"What's wrong with Carmen?" Joy asked. She had taken her cell phone to the break room.

140

After this morning's events, Todd felt it was best not to allow her to ride in with Joy. Carmen had been at work for over an hour and had not even turned her computer on. She sat quietly staring at the blank screen.

"What you mean?" Todd asked Joy.

"Something's up. She's not working."

"Maybe it's because we've paid you enough," Todd countered.

"Did she say something?"

"I'm talking about her bank account? What did you do?"

"Oh, that," Joy said nonchalantly. "I called and put a block on her account."

"How?"

"You're not the only who has her personal information. So I take it, our money came in."

Todd threw in the towel. "The only way we can get it is for her to go to the bank in person."

"Then it looks like we need each other."

* * *

Carmen sat the interoffice mail on one of the desks, then walked over to the plate glass window, leaned against the ledge, and watched the pedestrians as they strolled by. Several people rushed towards the bus stop with no time to spare. The city bus pulled up, they boarded, and as fast as it had come, it was gone.

Now that she thought about it, she should have turned on her computer, made it look like she was busy, but after this morning, there was no way she could have pulled it off.

She hurried out of the office and into the hallway, wasting no time as she made a mad dash for the elevator. She pressed the down button and paced nervously as she waited. Before the door fully opened, she squeezed inside. The rickety door hesitated then finally, it sealed her in and carried her to the first floor.

As the elevator door opened, the reception area came into view. Carmen quickly looked to her right at the hallway leading back to the office. The coast was clear. She then looked to her left at the glass barricade, the last obstacle to stand between her and the free world. She had no money, no coat, no excuses – she was leaving it all behind. As she rushed towards the door, she felt like she was in one of her dreams where the closer she got to her destination, the further it moved away. But this wasn't a dream, she was getting out even if it meant breaking through the glass to do it.

She clumsily grabbed the metal closure when she reached the door and pulled it towards her, swinging it wide open as if her life depended on it. Just as she lifted her foot to step out, Todd stepped in. In shock, her eyes fixed on his, Carmen didn't put up a fight. She simply stepped aside, almost absent mindedly, and allowed Todd to clear the door. A moment later, Joy came from behind.

"Take your stuff," Joy said, throwing Carmen's coat over the back of her head. "We're leaving."

* * *

"What's taking her so long?" Todd asked as he and Joy waited in the car for Carmen to come out of the bank.

"You shouldn't of let her go in by herself," Joy echoed as she nervously bit at her lip.

Todd would have accompanied her, but the security cameras prevented him from doing so.

With it being a Friday, the bank was busier than usual. When it was finally Carmen's turn, she followed a representative into one of the side offices.

"I'd like to set up a new account," Carmen said before the representative had finished pulling up her account. Although Todd knew nothing of her secret account, she wasn't taking any chances.

"You realize you have a negative balance on another account with this institution and . . . with an affiliate bank as well," the representative said as she viewed her information. "Funds will have to be diverted to pay those off first."

"How much?"

"A total of . . . $803.16."

"That's fine. And the balance I want it in the new account. Close the other one."

The representative set up a new account and had Carmen to sign all the necessary paperwork. After Carmen signed, she wrote her new account number on the inside hem of her cream top and tore the paperwork to shreds.

"Funds won't be available for another seven days," the representative said as she watched Carmen curiously.

"Can I pull money from the existing account?"

"Once you okay this transfer, no."

"Good. That's exactly how I want it."

* * *

When Carmen came out, it looked as if she was purposely taking her time like she didn't have a care in the world, but she was hurting. She felt like Doug had rammed his fist in her, like her uterus was going to fall out.

Carmen rolled her eyes at Joy as she strolled back to the car. Joy was laughing and rubbing her hands together like she had hit the jackpot. When she saw Carmen roll her eyes, she stopped.

"I know you did not roll your eyes at me," Joy turned and said after Carmen had climbed back in.

Carmen rolled her eyes again, this time exaggerating so there would be no question about it.

As Joy tried to unlatch her seat belt, Todd threw his arm across her chest.

"Girl, just drive!"

Joy put the car in gear and peeled off. Todd peered at Carmen through the mirror on the passenger side visor.

"What took you so long?"

Carmen looked at his reflection briefly then turned towards the window. "Paper work."

"You're lying."

Carmen looked at his reflection again. "Then call and ask them yourself! Dumb ass!"

Todd unbuckled his seat belt and leaned over the back of the seat. Carmen scooted to the other side away from his reach. As he tried to grab her, she kicked his arm. He grabbed her ankle. She screamed and kicked him in his face. Todd turned around in his seat.

"Stop the car!"

Joy looked at him and turned up her nose.

Todd felt his jaw. "Who the hell you cussing at? Wait till I get you home! You done lost yo' damn mind!"

Joy pulled into a parking space next to a moving truck. Todd jumped out and pulled Carmen out of the back seat, pushing her towards the apartment. Joy parked and got out as well.

"Where you going?" Todd asked her.

"I want to see that damn statement!"

Todd unlocked the apartment door and pushed Carmen inside. Joy followed. Before Joy shut the door, four men and three women followed her inside. Todd had just grabbed Carmen and was about to punch her in her face when he saw them.

"What the – "

"That's right, Todd. Thought you got away," Mario said as he walked up on him and slammed him into the wall. Carmen got out of the way.

Todd held up his hands. "I know what you're thinking, I had nothing – "

"Shut the fuck up!"

"Hey, I ain't got nothing to do with this. I don't even live here," Joy said, heading for the door.

One of the women got in front of her. As the woman came towards her, Joy walked backwards until she was standing with her back against the wall next to Todd.

Carmen tried her best not to look at any of Mario's cohorts. Her business was with him, not them. Besides, if it ever came back to bite her, she couldn't tell what she didn't see.

"Is this her?" Mario asked Carmen.

"Yeah, this is the Joy I was telling you about."

Joy's eyes left the woman and fell on Carmen. She looked at Carmen as if she had lost her mind. The woman turned Joy's cheek so that she faced her.

"You that heifer that used to beat up on my little cousin! Ah, shit! This gone be fun!"

Joy was scared to say anything.

"Carmen? So what's up?" Mario asked.

"Besides your weight equipment that you'll find in the second bedroom and your blender that's in the kitchen, everything in this apartment belongs to me."

Carmen then walked up to Todd. He looked back, with a nervous smile.

"Give me your keys."

Todd reached into his jacket and handed Carmen his set of keys. Carmen went into her bedroom and came back out with her accordion file after she had checked it to make sure her license and other documents were all accounted for. Carmen then came back and stood in front of Todd again.

"Your phone."

Todd reluctantly handed Carmen his phone.

"Right now I'm going to go to the library. Todd changed all my passwords to all my accounts. Whatever you're going to do to him, please wait until after I call you and he gives me the passwords. While I'm there, I'll let you know if he gave me the right ones."

"Don't worry. I got you," Mario assured her.

"Carmen, baby – "

Carmen looked into Todd's eyes. This was the last time she was ever going to see him.

"Just answer me one question," she said as her lips quivered. "Why me?"

In spite of the situation at hand, Todd looked back at her haughtily, his ego as unrelenting as ever. "Why not you?"

All Carmen could do was shake her head as Todd confirmed every suspicion she had about him. He never loved her, not the slightest. There was not a shred of remorse in him. It was the only time he had not lied to her.

Carmen then faced Joy. She stood toe to toe with her then snatched her special occasion hoops from her ears, tearing one of her lobes. It took everything Joy had not to react.

"Your purse."

As Joy slid her purse off her arm, Carmen grabbed it and dumped the contents on the table. She found her credit card. She then took all of Joy's cash from the paycheck she had cashed this afternoon. She looked at Mario, "Trust me, this is mine."

Carmen then took off Joy's wig and slapped it in her face.

"Please tell me that Joy is not the reason your head looks like that!" one of the women shouted.

Carmen shook her head.

"Oh, you done struck a nerve! Girl, get your stuff and get out! I got some work to do!"

"Carmen, baby, this is just a misunderstanding. Tell – "

"I told you to shut up! You better find a happy place and stay there!" Mario warned Todd as he tapped his bat across his hand. "And you put your hands on that? Oh, this gone be a long night."

CHAPTER 20

The day Carmen attempted to walk off her job was the day she stopped playing games with God. She stopped running from Him, owned up to the part she played in her dilemma, and allowed Him to help her face her fears. That same afternoon she called Mario. With all the crazy stuff going on in her life, it's funny how she had forgotten about him.

Mario believed that some situations were better dealt with on the streets. This was one time she agreed. Mario assured her that Todd was alive and that as long as she decided to stay in town, Todd would never bother her again. He also said that Joy and Todd spilled their guts. After they turned on each other, he had enough dirt on them both to put them away for a long time. Mario was only interested in their current offenses against him and Carmen. But if the need ever arose, he wouldn't hesitate in using what he learned against either of them.

Joy did talk too much. If she hadn't bragged on the fact that she helped Todd pick out her furniture, Carmen would have never thought to tip off her credit card company. They didn't move on it as fast as she thought they would, but since Joy was already in county, it probably didn't make any difference. Joy eventually found out who Doug was staying with and she shanked him. The paper listed him as being in critical condition.

After sorting through the papers in Todd's chest, Carmen discovered that Todd had no plans of leaving her any time soon. In fact she was the reason he dared to dream again. He needed the stability she provided him in order to jump start his career. She found where he had submitted an application to a regional bodybuilding competition. He too had a total of 90 days from the time he submitted his application to get his act together.

Carmen had been so locked into getting her money right that she couldn't see anything else. She didn't know when to cry uncle. The more she tried to climb out of the hole she dug for herself, the deeper she fell in. That was her weakness, she never exhausted her resources. At some point she had to finally wake up, recognize she was in over her head and put her trust in God.

She would have finished her 90 day probation, but since she was moving back home with her parents, she didn't qualify for the bonus. She said her goodbyes to Angie but Rosalind's whereabouts remained unknown. She sold her furniture, broke her lease and was on the next flight out.

She decided to finish her degree at one of the extension programs through her community college. Thanks to Todd, she had lost an entire semester. With another year of school and the credit charges Todd had incurred on her behalf, she figured she would owe just shy of $32,000 in student loans by the time she finished.

Children aren't their parents, but it doesn't stop parents from giving their children what they need. Her parents had given her a foundation upon which to build, but she didn't think the rules applied to her. Like so many young girls, she thought she could defy the odds.

"Hey Alicia! Where's Diane? . . . I have to be somewhere later this afternoon. I want her to go with me. . . . Yeah, tell her not to leave."

Carmen looked out the window as the plane dropped below the clouds.

"I need to get off, I'll be landing any minute. Love you. See you soon."

In three year's time she had compromised so much of what made her unique, all in an effort to be validated by others. She had only been concerned about today and refused to hear the voice of the 25 and 35 year old Carmen screaming out *take care of me* because the 19, 20, and 21 year old Carmen had done enough damage. Maybe at some point she'd forgive her, even tell her she had done well.

Meeting Todd accelerated what would have probably taken her the next ten to fifteen years to get. She could only hope when she got home that she could get through to Diane before she graduated and went off next year. Diane was as bull headed as she, destined to follow in her steps. Before she left, she took another pregnancy test. It was negative but she had developed two new symptoms, burning and itching. She scheduled an appointment with the health department before she left. She was convinced the STD test would be positive, the only thing she didn't know was for what or how many. She made arrangements for them to send the results back home. Diane didn't know it yet, but she was going with her to her appointment.

At this time, there were no lists. She had a lot of soul searching to do. A lot of healing. There was no justifying what she had been through, but she was able to go back home. Everybody didn't have that option. Every time she thought about Rosalind, she would be reminded of it. So as for now, she wasn't taking anything for granted like her hair for one. She had over an inch of new growth now. All but one of her patches had filled in completely. Angie talked about her natural journey. It inspired Carmen to get started on hers.

Carmen wheeled her luggage behind her as she looked for her exit. Winter semester was about to begin. Families were dropping their daughters off at the various terminals – some of them probably really nice girls. She spotted her parents waiting near the baggage claim area before they saw her. They were looking in the opposite direction. Tears gushed from her eyes the moment she laid eyes on them. Her mother was standing behind her father. He was in a wheelchair now.

Her parents were her foundation. They were her heroes, her strength. What they had was what she had left home to find. They sent her out whole and she was coming back battered, bruised – broken. They would be there to help her pick up the pieces. Even after she had been used, abused, turned out and pimped, she was their legacy, she was still their princess.

If I could go back and change anything about my life, just any one aspect, chances are good this book wouldn't exist. If my life hadn't unfolded the way it had thus far, I wouldn't have had the courage or determination to put my thoughts to paper for complete strangers to read.

There is a story in the book of I Kings of a widow during a time of drought who had only a handful of meal and just enough oil to make one last meal. Elijah the prophet came to her and requested that she make a cake for him before making the last for her and her son. She responded in faith and as a result, the barrel that housed her meal and the cruse of oil miraculously never emptied during the remainder of the drought. Prophetically, I have been told that writing is my cruse of oil, that it is the key to not only financial, but spiritual success. Somewhere along the road of hard knots, I began to believe it.

My name is Connie Barrett. I hail to you a native of Benton Harbor, Michigan, the third of eight children and the mother of two. I invite you to visit my website www.conniebarrett.com and follow me on my journey as I continue to branch into destiny.